RANA M̶A̶N̶C̶I̶N̶I̶

THE UNFINISHED BUSINESS OF

YOU + ME

BASED ON A TRUE LOVE STORY

Happy Easter Kaylyn!
Love, Mom
XO
2019

Some of the characters, incidents, and dialogue are drawn from the author's
imagination and are not to be construed as real. Any resemblance to actual events
or persons, living or dead, is entirely coincidental.

THE UNFINISHED BUSINESS OF YOU AND ME
Copyright © 2017 by Rana Mancini.
All rights reserved.
No part of this book may be used or reproduced in any manner whatsoever
without written permission.
For information email Rana@ChicTravelingMama.net

For my love.
Life without you wouldn't be a life at all. Thank you for
believing in me when I didn't believe in myself. And for
recognizing that being afraid of the dark is a real fear
(or so I've heard).

AUTHOR'S NOTE

The task of writing your life's story is daunting to say the least. It took me almost four years and several drafts. At first it was something I decided to do for myself. And maybe my kids and their kids. A fun story of sorts. Slowly it morphed into more, and now I can call myself a writer (I think).

This is a tale of heartbreak, twists, fate and a sprinkle of fiction.

It isn't told in chronological order as you might suspect. Although grade school is touched upon, the story doesn't stay there. The mention of it is pertinent, and I'm confident you'll think so too.

But this book is about more than finding true love. It's about the unfinished business of first love and if you've ever wondered what it would be like to get a second chance at love, this book is for you.

Thank you for coming on this journey with me.

We pick our partners because they represent the unfinished business from our childhood.
–Jay Pritchett (Ed O'Neill), *Modern Family*

PART I

♥ GROWN UP US – DECEMBER 24, 2008 ♥
#PLAYINGBYTHERULES

I didn't know how to respond, so I quickly blurted out what any self-respecting woman would, "I understand. I feel the same way."

The lie came spewing out of my mouth like the Niagara after a rainfall. I mean it's not like I could tell the truth. There were rules to uphold and the truth didn't really... well, belong there.

I couldn't help but wonder if this was punishment for all those times before... like some kind of sick payback perhaps?

I guess when you're the youngest of four in an Italian family, you learn to hold your own. "Vulnerability" was a curse word and being weak was not an option. I hadn't been 'the vulnerable one' in a relationship for as long as I can remember, and I was not about to start now.

"Good, I'm glad we're on the same page," he replied, as he handed me a Starbucks caramel latte-my favorite. "Oh, I almost forgot, I got this for you." He wore tattered jeans and a hooded sweatshirt, neither of which looked like they would keep him warm in the frigid December temperatures of northeast Ohio. With his perfectly trimmed beard and black beanie cap covering his slicked back hair, even dressed in casual clothes he looked simply stunning. God, why was this happening to me?

3

My stomach churned as I sipped my latte. Was it supposed to soften the blow? We had just had a fabulous night together, something I couldn't even bear to think about now. And the morning after, he gets me Starbucks then proceeds to drop this bombshell. What was happening?

"Well, we better get going. You don't want to be late and I need to finish my Christmas shopping," he said as he helped me up off his bed. "Do you have everything?"

"Yeah, I'm good," I said as I slung my purse over my shoulder. I looked around his room to be sure I was telling the truth. I didn't see any of my stuff, but so what if I left something behind? Maybe he'd find it later and it would remind him of me. Maybe he'd even miss me.

Never in my wildest dreams did I picture the morning turning out like this. I thought we would wake up in each other's arms, maybe spend the whole day together. I thought this meant something, something we could get excited about. But clearly, I was delusional. And now that my hopes were dashed, it was nearly impossible to act like my heart didn't just get ripped out of my chest. I have never been very good at keeping my feelings hidden; something that has gotten me into trouble a time or two. But, today, I had to Play. By. The. Rules. In some ways, I felt a sense of solace by falling back on the old relationship playbook. Frankly, it was all I knew: pretend you don't have the feelings you really have or risk humiliation. Never show your hand until you've seen theirs first was my hard and fast rule. And even then, it's a crapshoot. Better to just protect yourself by shutting up.

"That shirt looks better on you," he quipped, as he grabbed his wallet. "You should keep it."

I faked a smile.

4

I was wearing my skinny jeans and his sweatshirt so I didn't have to put my fancy blouse back on. Secretly, I had an overnight bag in my car containing a fresh outfit and a toothbrush; last night, I had wanted nothing more than this casual rendezvous to turn into a sleepover. After all, I drove an hour to his apartment in a mini snowstorm just to "hang out." It had been years since we sat and talked, and last night was just like old times, but better. I knew he would suggest that I just stay over instead of driving back home in the snow, but I acted like I shouldn't, of course. (I'd got that rule down). He even offered to sleep on the couch, so I could have the bed to myself. But I wasn't about to let that happen. "It's fine, we're both adults," I told him.

"Hey, I gotta put gas in my car across the street, why don't you meet me there? I'll pump your gas too, so you don't have to freeze your butt off in this cold," he said as we walked down his apartment steps.

As always, his charm matched his good looks. "It's fine. I'll do it later."

"No, really. I insist. It's literally across the street. You said last night your tank is on empty, right?"

Did I say that? Ah, just last night, before my world shattered... "Oh that's right. Well, great, thanks. Guess I'll see ya in a sec."

"Come on now, you know I'm always a gentleman," he said with a wink as he opened his building's front door.

Did he say that to all the women in his life? How many were there? I should have him pegged by now, but I seemed to be completely wrong. Stop. I needed to stop thinking about this and get out of here. Once I had some breathing room I could reassess. Talk to Laura. Figure things out.

We left his apartment building, and I stared at him as he headed to his sleek, black Alero. I had to keep up this façade for a few more minutes. It was almost over.

I just wanted to be alone so I could stop pretending like... I wasn't falling in love with him.

SPRING OF 1993, 4TH GRADE
#IfNotMeThanWho

Our Ohio neighborhood was a suburban wonderland. Populated with kids of all ages, I had plenty of playmates to choose from, aside from my three siblings, Joey, Elisha and Antonia, of course.

Being the youngest wasn't always a challenge. At first it was easy because everyone was eager to take care of me. I didn't have to do anything for myself, even speak. It became a bit more challenging after I grew up a little and began to assert my independence. Forming my own opinions made me a prime target. And man, do I have the scars to prove it.

Joey, the oldest, protected me. When he wasn't teasing me half to death that is. Elisha, the second oldest, always had a soft spot for me. That never changed. Antonia... well she was ruthless. Any aggression she had was taken out on me in the form of scratching, kicking and mocking. Despite that, we were still close. In relationship, age and proximity- we shared a room.

My parents were your average, hard-working suburbanites. My mother, at home (a job she kept until I was practically in middle school). The gourmet style dinners waiting for us in the evening were something I assumed every family got to enjoy. Homemade pasta was more regular than not and I'd put up a fuss if it was

7

Cavatelli and not Capellini. "It's the same thing but in a different shape," she would often assure me. It did not help.

My dad worked at the Ford Motor Company on the factory line. He didn't talk about it a lot except for when he was telling us the pranks he and his coworkers would play on each other. It was quite amusing from our angle when we'd quiz him at night to see what mischief they managed that day.

Summers consisted of riding bikes in the cul-de-sac, swimming in the Crippy's pool, jumping on our trampoline or playing night games of Jail Break.

I was nine. I loved watching Saturday morning cartoons and playing with baby dolls (although I didn't like to admit that to anyone other than Antonia who, even at eleven, was keeping the same secret). And so, what if I liked to pretend that certain boys from school were my husband when playing house?

The neighborhood parents, including mine, played cards all the time. Trying to sleep while six couples played euchre underneath the room my sister Antonia and I shared was next to impossible. I couldn't understand what was so much fun about cards—I could always hear my parents complaining afterwards about how they got stuck with the worst partner, but the food my mother cooked for the occasion more than made up for it.

Like true Italians, our Sundays consisted of sharing pasta with our extended family. Our first stop was Nonna and Nonno Petitti's for a huge lunch and then on to Nonna Mancini's for dinner. Although these gatherings were centered around food, eating was more of an afterthought for us kids. My cousins, especially Annabelle and Gia, were my closest friends. We'd hurry through our meal so we could play hairdresser in the basement or learn to play euchre with the adults. And we always did our best to avoid cleanup.

Because family was the focal point in my life, I didn't have a ton of friends at school.

Perhaps I didn't fit in because I begged my mom to make me shirts like this? She can't be blamed, I totally picked out that clown-themed fabric (I rocked that side pony though…).

I didn't really notice it until fourth grade when I was in Ms. Luciano's class. Most days I felt like an outcast. For my 'how-to' project early in the fall, I demonstrated how to make the infamous Italian cookie: pizzelles. I realized it was a bad idea when everyone complained that it reeked like black licorice. They were referring to the all-powerful anise oil, a key ingredient. I suppose it was potent, but I was more than used to it. Heck, pizzelles were a major food group in my family. Why didn't I remain sensible and demonstrate how a tornado works using a Pepsi two liter? Needless to say, I never lived that down.

Once I started hanging out with Laura, things started to get better. She didn't care that I came from a completely different family than the rest of our classmates. And she told me my pizzelle-making demonstration was her favorite. We talked about anything and everything, and she eventually became a part of my extended family. My cousins were always asking about her after she joined us for a few Sunday meals.

Fall turned into winter, and before I knew it, spring was upon us. In Ohio, this is a big deal because the winter drags on for what seems like forever. But with the weather warming up, flowers sprouting, and snow almost completely melted, all of us in the neighborhood were thrilled to get back outside for games of four-square and flashlight tag.

But more than just the weather was changing. I could feel things starting to shift for me at school one Monday morning after returning from spring break. Out of nowhere, five boys asked me to be their girlfriend! Now, never in a million years would I have pegged myself as the girl boys would want to date. I was shell-shocked. Brett, Justin, James, notes came pouring in instructing me to make a choice by circling one of three words: yes, no or maybe.

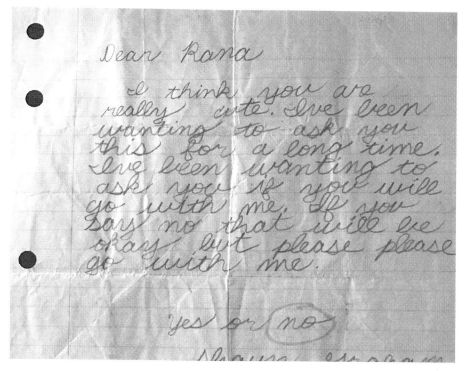

"Dear Rana I think you are really cute. I've been wanting to ask you this for a long time. I've been wanting to ask you if you will go with me. If you say no that will be okay but please please go with me."

This was from a sweet boy named, Shaun. One more 'please' and I might have caved.

The butterflies rose even higher in my stomach with each request. I had never received so much attention at once before—not at school or at home. As the youngest of four siblings, I was constantly lost in the shuffle. And at school, barely anyone except Laura had reached out to say hello. I found it thrilling to have someone, anyone, vie for my attention. But I still didn't totally understand it—was this a trick?

Then, at the end of the day I got an offer that had to be real; one that I couldn't refuse. And overnight, I was the envy of every girl at Powell Center Elementary. The hottest boy in school asked me to be his girlfriend right before I got on the bus to go home. He said it super casually, and in the blink of an eye it was over.

I was shocked, but I remained as cool as a cucumber. Although, more than likely it was because I didn't have time to react in any other way. And yet, as soon as those seven words, "What up? Wanna go out with me?" passed through *his* lips, my life would never be the same. Before I even knew what I was saying, I told him, "Yeah, sure."

Then, we both hopped onto our respective buses and were gone. And. So. It. Began.

♥ GROWN UP US – DECEMBER 24, 2008 ♥
#WalkOfShame

It took us about a minute to get to the Marathon gas station. I watched him in my rearview mirror while he pumped my gas. The cold air was making him fidgety. His athletic frame began to jump around like a boxer before he steps into the ring. I could see his warm breath hit the air as he pushed his left hand deeper into his sweatshirt pocket to get it out of the cold.

It was hard take my eyes away from him—he looked so amazing, like always. This was all turning out to be so unfair.

He put the nozzle back and came over to my window, "So, are you sure you know how to get there from here?" he asked.

Not a clue. "Yep," I replied.

"OK, cool...well maybe we can hang out again before you head back?"

"Yeah, maybe," I said.

"Well, shoot me a text and we'll get together."

"Sure."

"Have a Merry Christmas, Mancini. It was good seeing you again." He sounded sincere as he looked in my eyes. His were huge, piercing blue, with a remarkable ability to weaken your knees if you stared long enough. He leaned in and kissed my cheek. My heart skipped a beat as his scruff rubbed against my skin, reminding me of the night before.

"You too. I'll see ya," I replied, trying to sound perky. He watched while I rolled up my window and drove off. Did he seem sad we were parting ways? In my rearview mirror, I saw him start his car and pull out of the gas station.

As I turned for the on-ramp to I-71, I held back my tears, telling myself he could easily be driving right behind me right now—we were headed in similar directions.

I needed to talk to someone. My sister. Hell, with two young boys, she was one of the only people I knew who would even be up at this hour. I just needed a second opinion. Maybe cry, scream, or yell. Whatever! But first, where was my GPS? I had no idea where I was going.

"Calm down," Elisha said. Listening to my sister's soothing voice made me feel a little bit better.

"But really?! Can you believe he said that? I mean, why would he say that? It's not like I'm just some chick he picked up last night," I said.

"Rana, he's just scared. Trust me, he definitely has the hots for you," Elisha said. For a woman who's been off the market for four years, she really was knowledgeable about how single men behaved.

I entertained her idea, "Does he? Because he sounded so sure of what he was saying. I'm just so..." Tears started to fall, and I paused to regain my composure. Elisha was respectfully quiet. "I guess I didn't realize how much I cared about him."

"I know this sucks now, but I'm tellin' ya, it'll all work out. I have a feeling he's not going anywhere. I'm callin' his bluff," she said.

"Nah, you weren't there. His mind is made up. And I'll tell you one thing— "

"Shoot! Rana, I'm so sorry, I have to go, Sal just spit up all over himself. Call me later?"

"Sure, I understand. Well, Merry Christmas. Give the boys a kiss for me," I say, now getting sad that this year I wasn't going to see my sister and nephews for the holidays. They had just moved to Florida for my brother-in-law Stefan's recent promotion. It had taken me awhile to forgive him for taking her away from me, but the guy was pretty darn likable.

I remember when I met him. I was skeptical, mostly because I didn't *want* to like him. Our brother, Joey, had just gotten engaged to his college girlfriend and seeing my siblings grow up meant that I had to, too. So, I wanted the rest of us to stay single and continue having fun, like sisters in their twenties should.

But the night Antonia and I challenged Stefan to sing *Lady Marmalade* at karaoke—and he gladly accepted—I knew he was willing to do anything for Elisha. He earned my stamp of approval fair and square.

They're a great match. And really, he was the kind of guy I wanted for myself. Why was that too much to ask?

MAY 23, 1993- 4TH GRADE
#AllTheFeels

It was incredible; I still couldn't believe Ryan Cavanaugh and I were going out! I was his girlfriend and he was MY boyfriend. It had only been three days, but everyone knew. I tried to act as if this was something I was used to. Something I expected would happen. But who was I kidding? I didn't know the first thing about having a boyfriend of my own. Thankfully, only Laura knew that.

I almost didn't want summer to come. Sure, I'd be out of school, but when would Ryan and I see each other? Now, we saw each other at school every day, but my parents definitely wouldn't let that happen in the summer. But boyfriends and girlfriends had to hang out. If not, then how could they stay boyfriend-girlfriend?

Later that day when we got our yearbooks, I couldn't wait to go through it to find pictures of him or to fill out all my information in the front. Thankfully, Antonia had swim practice that night, so I could do all of this without her poking her head into my business. Because I shared a room with my sister, I had zero privacy when I wanted to talk to Ryan, - something that would change this summer when my brother Joey left for the University of Cincinnati and Antonia moved into his room. Thank God. But not even that could top being asked out by Ryan. It was by far the best part of my year.

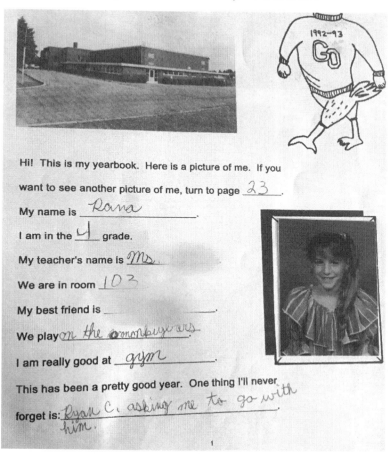

Hi! This is my yearbook. Here is a picture of me. If you want to see another picture of me, turn to page _23_.

My name is _Rana_.

I am in the _4_ grade.

My teacher's name is _Ms._.

We are in room _103_

My best friend is ____.

We play _on the monkeybars_.

I am really good at _gym_.

This has been a pretty good year. One thing I'll never forget is: _Ryan C. asking me to go with him._

Good ol' room 103, where my life transformed.
Also, a close-up of that awesome homemade shirt.

Because all the cool boys have a sideways smile.

♥ GROWN UP US – DECEMBER 24, 2008 ♥
#WTH

I pulled onto I-71 and began the trek to meet my brother. OK, so it sucked seeing her go. But what else was I supposed to do?

Last night was nothing short of amazing. *She* was amazing. It's no secret that I've always thought that. And after seeing her in the bar that night I was practically transported back to junior high or wherever this whole thing started.

But reliving this Rana thing is surreal. I thought the past was in the past. It probably still is, and last night was just a one-time thing. I mean, it's not like this could ever work between us. We've tried before, and it's just not meant to be. We'd be wasting our time, right? I mean we live thousands of miles apart. After our talk this morning, Rana obviously feels the same way anyway.

Then why can't I stop texting her? Speaking of, I better shoot her a text now and make sure she got to the market safely.

WHAT THE HELL IS MY PROBLEM?

FALL OF 1993, 5TH GRADE
#ReunitedAndItFeelsSoGood

"Hi," Ryan said as he approached me on the playground.

It was the first time I had seen him since late July when he left for vacation with his family. But he gave me his phone number on the last day of school so we could keep in touch over the summer. I felt obliged to give him mine, too, although it caused me to wait anxiously by the phone until he called in fear of my dad or Joey answering. I was relieved he only waited until the next day when I promptly told him I'd be the one to call from now on.

Did he still want me to be his girlfriend?

"Hi," I replied nervously.

"Hey. Soo, I got you something from Disney," Ryan said happily as he held his surprise for me behind him.

"You did?" I asked, surprised.

Ryan pulled out a stuffed Donald Duck from behind his back and handed it to me. Wow!

I felt just like my older sister, Elisha who had gotten flowers from a boy for her birthday.

This was so grown up—and I guess it meant Ryan was still my boyfriend.

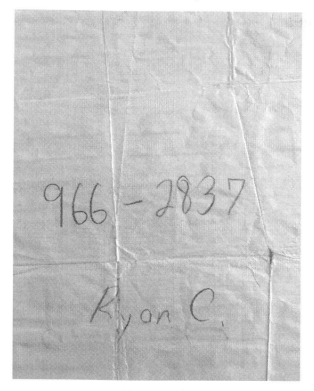

His original note. I opened and closed it just short
of a million times that day.

Ryan was always so cool. When he first arrived at Powell last year, his recesses were spent running from girls instead of playing sports with the other boys. He was also super cute, he had perfect hair, big blue eyes and he always wore jeans, not sweatpants like the other boys.

"Thanks," I said sheepishly. I was grinning from ear to ear but trying to stop—everyone else was watching us.

"You like it?" he replied.

"Yeah. He's cute," I said. Why did I just use the word 'cute?' 'Cute' made me sound like a baby.

"Cool. Well, see ya!"

And just like that, Donald and I were left standing next to the swings, our whole grade gawking. I looked down at the stuffed duck and pulled him into my chest. I knew he just earned a spot in my stuffed-animals-I-always-sleep-with collection.

The transition to fifth grade wasn't as scary as I thought. At first, I was worried because Ryan wasn't in my homeroom like last year. What girls would be sitting next to him? Would he forget about me? The possibilities had me reeling. I convinced myself he would dump me the second someone cuter came along. One day our teacher, Mr. Gallucci, prepped us for a new student that'd be joining our class. For weeks, I prepared myself for the possibility that Becky Dixon was going to win my boyfriend's heart. I was more than relieved when she arrived and blended in with everyone else.

And as the year progressed, I worried less. It became clear to me that Ryan was committed to being my boyfriend. He never talked about other girls or even looked at them, at least whenever I was with him.

But I wasn't comfortable with all the attention being Ryan's girl-friend brought. He didn't seem to mind so I pretended it didn't bother me, but I always felt like our classmates were staring at us. I just wasn't used to it.

Because of this, I was the most uncomfortable whenever Ryan tried to hold my hand. Only he didn't really hold it, he would just loop his pointer finger into mine. But one day, things moved way beyond hand holding, in a gesture so grand, it was history in the making.

♥ GROWN UP US – DECEMBER 24, 2008 ♥
#ItsNotMeItsYou

The West Side Market wasn't glamorous from the outside, but once you walked through the doors, its charm was undeniable. With huge pillars, a decorative ceiling and ancient architecture, you could tell it had been a bustling market for decades.

I felt my phone vibrate as I strolled in.

Hi, did you make it there ok?

Shoot, how do I answer this? Was my sister right? Either way, I wasn't in a place to respond right now. I felt confused as I shoved my phone back in my purse. Maybe if I ignored his texts he'd stop trying to contact me and I could move on with my life. But I knew that was easier said than done.

SPRING OF 1993, 5TH GRADE
#BUSTED

"It's causing a pretty big spectacle," Mr. Gallucci said softly, trying not to disturb my classmates who hadn't finished their spelling tests yet. Was it just me or was everyone listening to us instead of focusing on their papers?

"So, it uh, has to stop. Do you understand, Rana? We've spoken to Ryan already and he understands now. OK?"

"K," I replied staring down at my plaid skort.

This was SO embarrassing. I wished I could disappear into the floor. Was Mr. Gallucci going to tell my parents?

"Good, now go have a seat. We're reading silently until everyone is finished."

What Mr. Gallucci didn't know was that none of this was my idea. It was all Ryan's. I only gave him permission once. But now it was an everyday thing. And I don't know, I just never stopped it. Although it got a lot of attention, I guess I also kind of liked it.

The first time Ryan kissed me, I wasn't ready for it. School had just let out, and we were walking down the long, jam-packed hallway, surrounded by our classmates. Ryan stopped me right outside of the school doors and nervously asked, "Can I kiss you goodbye?" I wasn't even sure *what* exactly he was asking, but I said, "OK." I

24

quickly realized that what he meant wasn't a cheek kiss, it was a lip-to-lip kiss—something completely new for both of us. Immediately, I thought, I must be doing it wrong—my eyes didn't close like they do on TV; I've watched enough *Saved by the Bell* to know they should. As Ryan pulled away I could still feel some spit on my lips. I stood there, stunned, as he said goodbye and ran off to the bus.

Laura, who hadn't seen anything, caught up with me. "What's the matter?" she asked.

"Um...Ryan Cavanaugh just kissed me!"

"No way!" Laura shrieked.

I shushed her and we walked to our bus together. I had to get home and tell my sisters. They would never believe it.

After Mr. Gallucci called me out, I headed back to my seat as instructed. Craig Willoughby shot me a knowing glance, and the giggle under his breath had a ripple effect throughout the whole class. I looked around the room and was certain everyone knew what Mr. Gallucci just told me. I pulled my Baby-Sitter's Club book out of my desk, hoping everyone would get bored and stop paying attention. But I could hear the whispers spreading like wildfire. I turned to my bookmarked page and tried to be interested in Claudia's latest problems. I was sure they weren't as serious as mine.

Not kissing Ryan at the busses today wouldn't be a problem.

♥ GROWN UP US – DECEMBER 24, 2008 ♥
#BFF

I was feeling the consequences of not getting enough sleep last night at Ryan's, and the bustling market was making this even worse. I was amazed at how fast-paced everything was, considering it wasn't even 9AM. The vendors were positioned extremely close together, separated by glass cases that showcased their fresh food. Home-made staples represented a wide array of cultures: cannoli, falafel, tarte tatin, Moroccan tea, you name it. Everything smelled delicious, but today I didn't have much of an appetite.

I was here to meet my best friend Laura and help her sell bread for her fiancé's family bakery. She had asked for my help while I was home for the holidays and I had gladly accepted. It was a great way to spend some quality time with my bestie, and the extra cash didn't hurt either.

For most of the year, I was in L.A. working as a costumer on feature films. But movie production usually slowed down over Christmas and New Year's, so coming home was an easy decision.

I wasn't looking forward to filling Laura in on everything that had occurred between yesterday and today. Laura thought entertaining this relationship was a silly childhood fantasy that would never come true.

And I admit that, at first, it *had* seemed harebrained, but old feelings came rushing back the moment I laid eyes on him again.

Laura was setting out the fresh bread that had been packed in paper bags just hours before. It was still warm and smelled delicious.

"Hi," I said.

"Hey! Morning."

She was wearing comfortable but cute clothes. From the looks of it you'd guess that she was the fashion major. Her form-fitting yoga pants and bright white Nikes made me regret not changing into the clothes I had packed in my secret overnight bag.

We still had the same unbreakable bond we'd had since elementary school. Nothing shook it, not even me living halfway across the country. That's why I cherished whatever time we had together.

"You look tired."

"Aw, thanks," I replied sarcastically, putting my drink down and lending a hand with the bread.

"Come on, I didn't mean it like that. Somethin' wrong?" she quizzed.

Her long dark hair was pulled into a loose bun on the top of her head and it looked effortlessly cute. Even without a stitch of makeup Laura was pretty. Half Greek and half Italian, she had lighter skin like mine, but without a blemish in sight. She didn't realize how lucky she was to not have to worry about pimples. I had to work hard at maintaining my complexion and didn't get results nearly as good.

"Oh, I don't know," I hesitated.

But knowing it was going to come out eventually, I continued. "I spent the night with him last night..." I turned away from her and started putting scones in the front case. I could feel her eyes burning a hole through the back of my head.

"You what?!"

Expecting her judgment, I quickly turned to face her. "Relax, nothing happened."

"Yeah, right!"

"Ok well, yes... And no," I said in confusion.

Raising her eyebrows, she waited for me to continue. But I wasn't sure I could. The whole morning had spun out of control and seemed like a huge blur now.

"It's complicated," I said frowning.

"Come on, try me," she said empathetically as she continued loading the bread.

Now that Laura was officially off the market, she looked to me to provide her with a healthy dose of relationship drama. Amid planning their big, fat Greek wedding, Matt and Laura were a perfect pair in a lot of ways. For one thing, his family's bakery was rapidly expanding and it suited Laura. She was quickly becoming a self-taught pastry chef —and a good one at that.

"Well, remember when I made plans with him to hang out yesterday?" She nodded.

"I couldn't get up to Cleveland until like, 9-ish because I was waiting for the storm to calm down a little," I started. December in Cleveland could be considered one giant blizzard.

"Yeah."

"So, I got there and he was wrapping gifts for his little sisters," I said, full well knowing that this was going to illicit the he's-such-a-sweetie response.

"Aw, that's cute."

"Yes, he's cute," I said sarcastically.

"Why do you say it like that?"

"Because, everything was going great. We had a beer, looked at old photos, and spent hours just catching up on each other's lives. I even turned on the heavy flirting," I said closing the glass cases and turning on the register.

"What'd you do?" Laura smirked.

"I made sure I touched his arms as we thumbed through the picture albums, and we even got into a mini snowball fight in his living room with the snow from his balcony. I mean I made *sure* it crossed the friend-line."

Laura and I both knew that getting or, even worse, *staying,* in the friend-zone was one of the worst places to be. Crawling out of it would be an uphill battle. It was critical to establish from the beginning that two people look at each other as more than friends.Laura giggled.

"OK, and?"

"Well, then it got to be late and it was still kind of snowing. Since the market is close to his house and the storm could have gotten worse, he suggested I just stay the night. But, ya know, I acted all like, 'oh, I couldn't, I should go' type-stuff, but then I obviously agreed to it."

"Right, right," she laughed.

"So, he asked me if I would be more comfortable if he slept on the couch," I lowered my voice to be sure none of the other market vendors nearby could hear me.

"Yeah, and what'd you say?" Laura asked. She took a seat on one of the wooden stools behind our small stand as I flopped down on the other.

"Well, I told him 'don't be silly!'"

We burst into laughter! This was all part of the elaborate game we would find ourselves playing. We always knew, the unspoken code: if a woman wants to be considered long-term material, then she had to make sure she doesn't come off slutty. And since wanting a woman to stay the night doesn't make a man look easy, accepting the invitation too eagerly would certainly have negative implications. A true double standard if I've ever seen one, but we both knew it was true.

"So, you both slept in his bed?" Laura asked in a whisper. Unlike me, Laura knows the other vendors well because she sells at the market twice a week.

"Yeah. I told him we were both adults and it would be fine and yadda, yadda. And so, we lay there talking for a while. But then we had this little bet going, and—"

"Wait. A bet? What *kind* of bet?" she interrupted.

"Oh, I don't know, I mean, I just said..." My phone vibrated in my purse. Laura looked at me.

"Is it him?" she asked.

I sighed as I looked at my phone.

"Yeah, it's him all right."

Laura sat up on the edge of her stool. "What's it say?"

I held the phone up so she could read the text.:

Hello???

She looked at me, perplexed. I sighed and sipped the Starbucks latte I had brought in with me from the car. Remembering where I got it gave me a pit in my stomach. I spotted a nearby trashcan and chucked it in. The last thing I needed was a latte laced with pity.

NOVEMBER 23, 1994, 6TH GRADE
#MissYouAlready

"Rana!" Ryan shouted down the hall.

It was the day before Thanksgiving, and the long weekend ahead was making us restless. As the dismissal bell rang, we all made a run for it.

I stopped in the hallway and turned around to look for him.

I heard the occasional, "Bye, Rana!" or "Happy Thanksgiving!" sprinkled throughout the vast sea of kids darting by. I spotted Ryan.

"Hey!"

"Hey, I wanted to give you something before you got on the bus," Ryan panted.

I was intrigued.

He opened up his backpack and pulled out a folded note. "But don't read it now. Wait until you're by yourself."

Whoa. "Sure, OK. Thanks," I said slipping the note into my coat pocket.

"Have a nice Thanksgiving. Maybe we can meet up sometime soon and go to the mall or go skating or something," he said.

"Yeah. That'd be nice. I mean, cool. That'd be very cool," I replied correcting myself.

"Ryan and Rana sittin' in a tree! K-I-S-S-..." a group of 7th grade boys chanted as they scampered down the hall.

31

Ryan rolled his eyes.

"Come on, we better get going,' he said as he grabbed my hand and walked me to my bus. He gave me a hug and whispered in my ear, "Don't forget to read my note."

Feeling his breath on my skin sent chills all over my body. I watched him as he disappeared into the chaos. My heart ached. I hated saying goodbye to Ryan, even if it was only for a few days.

I hopped on my rowdy bus and spotted an empty seat near the back. I waved to a few friends who I would normally sit with, but today I want to be alone to read my special note. I plopped down on the dark, vinyl seat and opened it.

"Love ~~You~~/ With Love Ryan Cavanaugh" I guess he didn't have an eraser and thought I wouldn't notice. Girls (a.k.a. detectives) see everything.

"Whoa," I panted as I cradled the note to my chest.

♥ GROWN UP US – DECEMBER 24, 2008 ♥
#KissAndTell

"What's all this mean? And what bet?!" Laura asked losing her patience.

"OK, the bet: So, we were lying in bed and I bet that he wouldn't kiss me. I know, stupid, right? But it was part of my 'heavy flirting' agenda."

Laura nodded as she took a swig from her water bottle.

"I mean I *know* how competitive he is. I knew he wouldn't be able to resist. And I was right. He kissed me. And we made out for like...an hour?" I said contemplating. Truth is, I had no idea. It could have been three hours for all I knew. Time flew by and neither of us seemed to mind.

"And?"

"And then we finally fell asleep..."

"Whoa, wait—you slept over at his place, made out for an hour and...that's all?" Laura asked in disbelief.

"Yep."

"You're such a liar!" she exclaimed as she threw her water cap at me.

"No, I'm not! I swear," I exclaimed dodging it.

"So, what's with all of the texts then? Did you guys get in a fight or something?"

"Ha. No. Not exactly, he...said something this morning that freaked me out. Something I wasn't expecting."

"Really? Like what?" Laura quizzed.

"He," I began, "He said he liked me and everything, but he wasn't looking for a, uh, 'relationship,'" I sputtered.

Laura's face sank. "Oh. Ouch."

"Yeah," I sulked.

"Excuse me, can I have these two loaves?" asked an older lady pointing to the case. Completely caught up in conversation, we hadn't even noticed her. Did she just hear my humiliating admission?

As Laura bagged her purchase, I glanced in the trashcan and saw the latte I had just thrown away. Man, this sucked. Ryan Cavanaugh had never hurt me like this before. But I guess everything was different now; he was a man and not the boy I once knew.

While the woman waited for her change, she shot me a compassionate smile. "Don't worry honey, you can do better," she winked.

"Oh, why, thank you," I replied sarcastically enough for only Laura to pick up on. The woman left and I turned back to Laura.

"'Do better,' huh? How many times over the years have I tried to convince myself that there's somebody better than him?"

"Hmm, lots?" Laura appeased me.

"Yep. I was wrong every time!"

PART II

SPRING OF 1996, 7TH GRADE
#WhatAreFriendsFor

"But he's the cutest guy in school. And you just tossed him like he didn't even exist." Laura had a way of pointing out the obvious.

We had both taken her bus home from school so we could work on our history project together. But somehow, this was more interesting than Eleanor Roosevelt's life story.

"I know, I know. You've already told me that, Laura. But what was I supposed to do? I don't want to be his girlfriend anymore."

"Okay, I'm just saying, like two girls asked him out this week alone," Laura said a little too loudly, bobbing her head to Tupac's, *I Ain't Mad at Cha*.

Laura rummaged through her backpack for our project instructions. Her thick ponytail was held perfectly in place by her white scrunchie, complimenting her jean shorts and oversized Calvin Klein tee. I was basically wearing the same thing, but in different colors. It was practically our 7th grade uniform.

"Really? What'd he say?" I asked, hoping I didn't sound too eager.

"Um, he said 'no' I think. Wwwwhy?" Laura asked in amusement.

"Uh, I don't know. Just wondering. I mean he can totally go out with whoever he wants. Totally." I looked up at her to see if she was buying it.

"Right. Good, because I heard he's finally going to ask someone out. Can you believe it?" Laura said, looking at herself in her powder compact.

"Are you serious?" I said slamming my notebook shut a little too loudly. "That's crazy. Like, wow. Who is it? Do you know? And who told you that?" I said, no longer caring how eager I sounded.

I was firmly standing by my decision to break up with Ryan, but I was never sure I had done the right thing. Especially when my friends constantly pointed out how cute and sweet he was.

But the truth was, I needed a break from the constant gossip. Even though we were now in middle school, it still felt like all the attention was laser-focused on our relationship, more specifically, when we would have our first French kiss. Now, letting Ryan stick his tongue in my mouth was something that I wanted to do, I really did, but I was terrified—would I do it right? Would my nose get in the way? What side would I turn to? It was easier to just reject him when he asked, which turned out to be a lot. And, ultimately, the pressure got to be too much. I needed to get away from it and was easier to just walk away.

I could tell Ryan wasn't sure about the break-up, but I didn't give him much of a choice.

It was always possible that we would get back together, but I hadn't been ready to make the leap yet. However, Ryan actually *wanting* and *pursuing* someone was new. And it made me feel more jealous than I cared to admit. I was used to Ryan only wanting me. Even if I didn't reciprocate those feelings, I certainly didn't want him finding someone who did.

But I had noticed he was distracted by the new crop of girls fresh on his trail. They even included sixth graders and older girls who didn't even know his name yet. They were so obnoxious about it too. "Ohmygod, I was just in study hall with the cutest guy, I think he's actually like, a seventh grader!"

I mean, how annoying.

But being apart from Ryan gave me a chance to focus on my friends, like Laura. Plus, I wanted the option to go out with other boys who were interested in me as well. There was a world outside of Ryan Cavanaugh, and I wanted to see it for myself. I wanted to be more than just Ryan's girlfriend.

"Jesse told me that Shannon told her that Ryan has the hots for Emily Watson. She just broke up with Shane Flynn— "

"Wait! Emily Watson, as in eighth-grade-Emily-Watson?" I interrupted in amazement. The only thing worse than him moving on was him moving on with one of the prettiest eighth graders at Munson.

"Yeah. Ryan has the same study hall as her in second period. They sit right next to each other and— "

"All right, all right! I get it, Laura. He likes her and she likes him-end of story!" I went from lying down on her floor to standing on my knees practically shouting. There was no hiding that I was genuinely upset about this.

"Whoa. You asked, remember?" Laura snapped back.

"I know, I know. Look, I'm sorry. I'm just..."

"You totally still like him!" Laura laughed as she threw her Popple. It hit me square in the face. Irritated at first, I was glad she broke the ice.

I threw it back and giggled. "Ow! Do not!" Calmed down, I lay back down on the floor.

Laura slid down the side of her bed to get eye level with me. "Yes, you do. Rana, you really still like him...don't you?" She turned serious.

My giggles turned to silence, and I looked away from her. The truth is, I didn't know how to answer. Laura's five-disc CD player started to click around, changing CDs. Take That's, *Back for Good* started playing. I rolled my eyes at how appropriate it was.

I turned to face Laura who was waiting patiently for my answer but I think my tears said it all. My need to be free from everything Ryan had come full circle.

"Oh Rana..."

About a month later the yearbooks we ordered in September finally arrived, which was always an exciting time. The thrill of getting your yearbook signed by all your friends, exchanging it with your besties during study hall, taping blank sheets of paper in the back because some of your friends took up an entire page to tell you what an awesome time they had with you this past year. It was almost always wrapped up with the ever popular: S.T.S. (stay the same) or K.I.T. (keep in touch). And if you were *really* close, you let your best friends take your yearbook home with them for a night so they could write something long and thoughtful and reference all your inside jokes.

"Hey," Ryan said as he approached our lunch table. The cafeteria was crowded, noisy and reeked of chocolate milk and fried food. Occasionally the girls and I would sit with our guy friends, but other times we sat solo. I'm not sure what it depended on, but today was one of those days we just wanted to be with the girls. And I was happy to be able to chat with my friends without the pressure of having to look cool in front of the boys.

"Hi," I replied as everyone turned their attention toward us. I quickly swallowed the bite of my ice cream Snickers bar I had just taken.

Ryan and I hung out with all the same people, so I knew that he had just dumped Emily Watson. But none of our friends could get a straight answer as to why. "I don't know, just because," he would say.

I had finally moved on and just started dating Anthony Lucarelli. He was the 'Ryan Cavanaugh' at our rivalry middle school, Craigsville. Everyone knew him mostly because, like Ryan, he was Craigsville's sports stud. All our guy friends thought of him as the enemy either because Craigsville had just beaten our basketball team or because they felt I belonged with Ryan. Either way, it annoyed me.

They would tease me and say things like, "What, is no one at Munson good enough for you, Rana?" Or, "Out of all the guys in the world, you have to pick *him*?"

They weren't *really* mad at me; actually, I had a lot of wonderful friends (both guys and girls). We were a large group, but with surprisingly little drama, aside from the stuff with Ryan and me.

"So, did ya get your yearbook yet?" he asked, ignoring my girlfriends. Approaching a table full of girls didn't really faze Ryan Cavanaugh like it would most boys. He knew any one of them would fall over at the chance to go out with him.

"Yeah, I did. But Laura has it right now in study hall," I replied.

"K. Well, I want it when she's done. I can get it from her in English and give it back to you in history. Cool?" Ryan asked. He tended to phrase things in a way that made it seem like I had a choice, when really, I didn't.

"Sure. I mean, if you want," I said hoping I sounded smooth in front of my friends.

"Yep. I'll see ya in history, Mancini." And he strutted off to-wards the lunch line.

I watched intently, innocently staring at his butt. I could see his plaid boxers sticking out ever so slightly from the long jean shorts he had on. His striped Polo shirt was crisp and clean per usual. His hair was shiny from all the gel he used to mold it into its spiky shape every morning. It never looked any different at the end of the day. Not even when he played basketball. At the end of a game, it hadn't moved an inch—I was watching all winter, cheering him on from the sideline.

"Uh, Rana?" asked my friend Holly who was sitting across the table.

"Huh? What?" I said snapping out of my daze.

"You're totally staring at him!" she said as everyone started to laugh.

"Um... busted?" I said poking fun at myself.

Two periods later in history, I found my seat right next to Laura and plopped down.

"Hey, did Ryan— "

"Get your yearbook from me?!" Laura asked eager to fill me in on the juicy details.

"Right! He came up to me at lunch and was all like, 'Hi, I'm tak-ing your yearbook from Laura.'"

"Totally!" she giggled. "He came into English and was like, 'Hey, give me Rana's yearbook so I can sign it.' And then I was like, 'Well, did you ask her' and all this stuff and he was like 'Yeah, it's cool, she wants me to have it and give it back to her in history.'" Laura said, lowering her voice to do her best boy impression.

"What? I never said I *wanted* him to have it. He asked *me*. He can be so— "

"Shhhh! He's coming" Laura whispered as the bell for 11th period rang.

Ryan strolled in and took the only empty seat in the class, which, of course just happened to be two seats behind mine. It made me fidgety.

As Mrs. Fulkner began class reminding us of our upcoming papers due next week, Stephanie Ratler tapped me on my shoulder. I turned around and she handed my yearbook to me with a shrug.

I looked back at Ryan who was staring at me. He gave me the same sideways smile he did whenever he was pleased with himself. He looked so cool and, dare I say, sexy whenever he did it.

He winked. A wave of excitement washed over me.

"Uh, Miss Mancini?" Mrs. Fulkner said with a stern voice. I snapped my head back towards the front of the class. I heard Ryan snicker.

"Please pay attention, this is important," she said as she went back into describing what a 'good' paper would contain.

I glanced over at Laura who saw the yearbook on my desk.

"What's it say?" she mouthed.

I opened it up and thumbed through until I saw his neat handwriting. Ryan had unusually good penmanship for a boy. His cursive was prettier than most girls (something that always scored him points with our teachers).

He left it short but sweet:

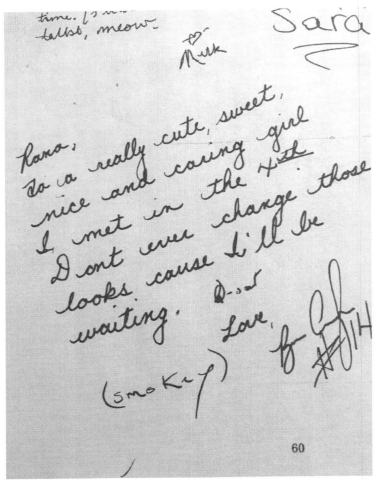

"*Rana, To a really cute, sweet, nice and caring girl I met in the 4th. Don't ever change those looks cause I'll be waiting. Peace-out Love, Ryan Cavanaugh #14 (Smokey)*"

"Well?" Laura whispered.

A smile came across my face as I shut the book. I felt Ryan's eyes one me. I felt confident. Bold. The burning question I wanted to know ever since our breakup last year had just been answered. Exhale.

44

After history Ryan gave me his yearbook to sign. Jeez, how do I follow that? I wondered.

As our science teacher put on a VHS of the Galapagos Islands, I started my spiel to Ryan. He sat in the front row of the class and I liked that I could see him but he couldn't see me. It made it easier to get my thoughts out on paper. I fumbled around with my purple pen before finally starting to write:

Can you tell I'm having second thoughts? Just a little?

"Ryan, To a sweet, <u>cute</u>, sensitive guy I've known since the 4th grade. You have the cutest little sisters. I'll be cheerin you on in b-ball and football. (Hopefully)"

45

"I'm glad you'll be waiting. Don't wait too long. Well, you can if you want. I can't believe I'm turning you down. You were the 1ˢᵗ guy I truly liked. You got all the gals. Call me always. I'll be waiting I like hearing from you. But don't hang up on me. love ya always Rana"

There. I think that's good enough. Got my feelings out for him but still in a friend-way. Right? Talk about complicated, sheesh.

SUMMER OF 1996, GOING INTO THE 8TH GRADE
#UnluckyLucarelli

"Anthony looks so cute tonight, Rana," said Holly, giving me a nudge.

The other girls chimed in with agreement while all I could do was giggle.

She obviously couldn't tell he was less than excited to come as my date. And understandably so. Being the only person who didn't go to Munson, he felt a little outnumbered. The strain between him and our guy friends was something we all felt, but Anthony wasn't going to let me come alone. Especially when Ryan was going to be here.

We were at Mary's house celebrating her 13th birthday with a bunch of our friends. Like most get-togethers, we weren't mingling with the boys just yet. Instead, we watched them shoot hoops in the driveway.

They were right. Anthony's dark hair was slicked back, and he wore a fresh t-shirt with shiny Jordan high-tops and long jean shorts. His plump lips and exotic cologne were my kryptonite. He was 100% Italian like me and had light olive skin. In short, he was exactly what I wanted in a boy, physically speaking. And when you're in junior high, looks rule over personality. Heck, they rule over everything.

"Yeah, but did you see Ryan? I mean, wow," Natasha proclaimed. She always seemed to comment on what a stud Ryan was, making me paranoid she had a thing for him. And, if so, that one day she would act on it.

Natasha's thick, straight blonde hair was annoyingly shiny. It always seemed like she was trying too hard. Today, she had on the shortest shorts, with a thin, spaghetti-strapped tank top. And of course, her pink bra straps were showing, like always. Yuck.

Laura shot her a dirty look that made me smile. You could always count on your bestie for things like that. I looked at Laura and nodded knowingly.

I turned around to watch as Anthony and Ryan casually dribbled around one another, shooting each other the occasional glare. They were like two wrestlers dancing around the ring waiting for contact. You could cut the testosterone with a knife.

"Hey," Anthony said as he approached the girls.

"You look good out there." I said, letting him know I was on his team.

Anthony was full of self-assurance, but in a more arrogant and prideful way. He was the kind of guy who knows just how good-looking he is—very different from Ryan. But he also had a sweet side and, at times, if we were alone, he even let it show.

Anthony was also a mama's boy at heart. His older siblings got into trouble and experimented with drugs the way a lot of teenagers do. But Anthony was different. Being both a great student and a superb athlete, it was clear he would get a scholarship and go to a good college. Anthony's family talked all the time about his future college prospects. At my family's dinner table, we talked about the most recent episode of *ER*.

"We're gonna start a game in a few minutes, two-on-two. Want to come over and cheer me on?" he said as he gave me a wink.

I chuckled and assured Anthony I'd be rooting for him. He pointed to his cheek meaning I was supposed to kiss him. As I did, I could feel Ryan watching the whole thing. He made me feel like I was doing something wrong, but I quickly brushed the thought aside. Anthony was my boyfriend, and Ryan and I had been broken up for a long time.

"Hey, Anthony! You playin' or what, man?" Ryan yelled.

Anthony smiled at me before turning around and enthusiastically shouting back, "Let's do this! Who's on my team?"

"Ben is. Ben, you're with Anthony," Ryan said with a snide smile.

Anthony looked at Ben and all the enthusiasm drained from his face.

Ben was slender and a lot shorter than Anthony. He didn't have a competitive bone in his body and only played basketball because all his friends did. Athletic wasn't the word I would use to describe him.

"Sweet bro, and you're taking..." replied Anthony sarcastically waiting for Ryan's answer.

"It's me and Farelli," Ryan quipped as he glanced at Anthony.

Mike Farelli was the second-best player on Munson's basketball team, next to Ryan, of course. He was not only tall, but he had ups, dribbling skills, and plenty of coordination, things that didn't always come naturally when you're that big.

Anthony looked Mike up and down, and knew this game would be an uphill battle.

Ryan threw the ball at Anthony's chest to indicate that the game had just begun.

49

"OK, here we go!" shouted Ryan.

Anthony was on Ryan the entire time, but Ryan was clearly the better player. He dribbled past Anthony like a man on a mission and even stripped the ball from his hands countless times. Anthony's face was turning red, and I don't know if it was because of the heat or anger. I couldn't hear everything they were saying, but I could tell they were exchanging jabs the entire time. I winced as Ryan ducked around Ben to set up for the three-pointer that won the game.

In the end, Anthony and Ben didn't really stand a chance. Ryan and Mike were just too good. The game ended with an eight-point gap.

"Good game, Lucarelli" Ryan said sincerely as he looked Anthony's way. I thought Ryan was still being a good sport, one of the reasons why he was frequently captain of any team he was on.

Anthony starting heading my way, ignoring Ryan. He gave me a kiss on the cheek and took a swig from the Pepsi I was holding.

"Fair game, don't you think?" Anthony said sarcastically. "I mean, Ben? The kid couldn't shoot if his life depended on it."

"Anthony, Ben isn't that bad," said Holly, who was sitting beside me. She and Ben had been good friends since elementary school.

"'Isn't that bad'? Open your eyes, Holly. Ryan stole the ball from him like twelve times," Anthony quipped.

"Maybe you didn't lose because of Ben. Maybe you lost because Ryan is better than *you!*" Holly blurted out. She stood quickly and took a can of Mountain Dew over to Ben who was plopped down next to Ryan. In typical Ben fashion, he was laughing off the thrashing.

Anthony looked stunned. Holly usually wasn't very good at standing up to people, why did she have to start now? I rolled my eyes. Laura shot me an empathetic glance as she headed over to get Mike a drink from the cooler.

I had to try and diffuse the situation.

"Anth, don't worry about it. Holly didn't mean it."

"Yeah whatever... You ready to go yet?"

"But Anthony, we like, just got here," I moaned.

"Well, this party's lame. Plus, now we have time to go back to my house and watch a movie," Anthony said trying to convince me.

Clearly, Anthony's ego was too bruised to stay. So, I reluctantly agreed.

"Sweet. I'm gonna call my mom to come get us" he said. As Anthony went inside to use the phone, my gaze shifted to Ryan who was still dribbling around the court. He shook his head in disapproval.

I felt like a sell-out. Why could Ryan push my buttons like this? Why did I care so much about what he thought of me?

I'm with Anthony now. He's cute. And cool. And so, what if Ryan can beat him in basketball? Anthony is what I want. What I need. And Ryan Cavanaugh can just shove it!

As I was thinking this, Natasha came up from behind Ryan and stole the ball. She giggled as she danced around taunting him to steal it back. Ryan was amused and played along. Suddenly, leaving didn't seem like such a bad idea after all.

"Hey! Let's snap a few pictures!" Mary's mom shouted, coming out into the yard. "Mary, come on!"

We all gathered in an awkward group in the backyard and waited for a group picture. "Come on, you guys clump together," Mary's mom commanded. As we gathered to pose for the picture, somehow, Ryan and I ended up next to each other. With Anthony still inside, Ryan grabbed my hand behind my back and gave it a squeeze. I was shocked and surprised, but it made me smile. Everything I had just been thinking about Anthony and Ryan started to melt away. Somehow, this moment just felt right.

There's that sideways smile again. Got me every time...

SUMMER OF 1996, GOING INTO THE 8TH GRADE
#LuckyLucarelli

"Is that Anthony Lucarelli?" Mike asked.

"Yep, it is," I said with a sigh of annoyance.

"She actually brought him to the party?" Ben chimed in.

"Obviously, yeah."

"Great, now we'll have to school him in basketball," Mike quipped as he bumped my arm.

I watched them walk into the party hand in hand. Rana began to hug her girlfriends and greet everyone while he just stood there like a dumb statue. I knew they were going out, but I didn't have to be a witness. It's not like they could flaunt it in the school halls, since he didn't go to Munson. But now it was right in front of my face. I kept my expression blank as he walked my way. He was on my turf now.

"Hey man, what's up?" Anthony said approaching me with his hand held out.

I reluctantly took it and gave him a nod, "Sup."

"Boys," Anthony said raising his hand in the air to all the guys.

We were over at Mary's for her birthday, about to shoot hoops. She lived on a quiet cul-de-sac. Balloons were tied to the mailbox, streamers decorated the garage and a picnic table with plenty of chairs were scattered throughout her lawn. The girls were all hanging out near the garage, but us guys, we stayed close to the hoop.

Anthony's arrogance bothered me. *He* bothered me. And it wasn't because Craigsville just beat us in basketball. Rana was always quick to dismiss his attitude and say what a great guy he was. And *that* was starting to bother me. Why couldn't she see what a major tool he was?

Maybe the guys were right. Maybe I still liked her. But it didn't matter if that creep, Anthony was in the picture. Plus, I was sick of convincing her that we were great for each other. I always saw her for who she really is: strong and smart and cute. SO cute. But now she felt like she had something to prove. Like if she dates other guys, she'll show everyone that she can be somebody without me. Why doesn't she realize that I feel like a nobody without her?

But I didn't want to think about this now, I wanted to have fun tonight. Besides, Eddie told me that Natasha had a thing for me. And that kind of piques my interest.

"Guys, are we starting a game, or what?" Eddie asked as he threw the basketball at my chest.

I caught it, "Yeah, man, we'll play right now. But I think Anthony wants in. Hey, Anthony! You playin' or what, man?" I yelled his direction. Anything to separate those two.

"Fine, me and Dave got winners," Eddie said as he plopped down in the grass.

We were giving Anthony a proper Munson butt-kicking, and I was loving every second of it. I could feel Rana staring at us, and for a minute I was tempted to let him win. For her sake. But Mike wouldn't allow it, he had an agenda all his own. Pretty sure he wanted to look good for Laura. And show Anthony that the only reason Craigsville beat Munson was because of the lucky shot Anthony made to end the game. "Lucky Lucarelli," that's what we called him behind his back.

Anthony guarded me closely as I took it to the hole and made another lay-up. I winked at him and passed him the ball so they could start at the top of the key.

"Watch it man, you threw that hard," Anthony winced.

"My bad, got carried away," I replied. It was the truth. I was hype. But I also wanted him to know whose turf he was on.

"OK, bro. I just hope it's not because I got the girl and you didn't!" he said as he crossed me up and stepped back to swish a jumper. Another lucky shot for Lucarelli.

I held my composure, "Nah man, it's not that at all. But I understand if you're mad because you're losing," I replied sarcastically.

"We didn't lose to you during the season did we, Cavanaugh?"

"Whoa, what's the problem here guys?" Mike stepped in to ease the tension. Ben was quick to jump in right behind him.

"Nothing's the problem. L.L. is just bent out of shape over the score," I wisecracked.

Ben and Mike chuckled.

"What's with the L.L. stuff?" Anthony sighed getting more agitated.

"Nothin' man. Nothin' at all, now can we play?"

"You've got a real problem, Cav."

"Let's just hurry up. Eddie is waiting for me to beat him next." And with that, I blew past Ben to plant my feet for a three-pointer to end the game. In your face, Lucky Lucarelli.

After taking the loss, Anthony disappeared inside to nurse his wounds. "My mom wants us to take some pictures guys," Mary hollered.

"No prob, happy birthday, Mary," I said giving her a hug.

"Thanks, Ry."

As Mary's mom clumped us together, I ended up next to Rana. Maybe I did it on purpose, but either way, I was glad.

She smelled delicious. Before I knew what I was doing, I touched her hand behind her back. To my surprise, she grabbed my hand and squeezed it. How could she deny there was still something between us?

♥ GROWN UP US – DECEMBER 24, 2008 ♥
#LoveKnowsNoBoundaries

"Well what about this whole last month and a half of talking on the phone and texting you every day and all that stuff? He waited this long to tell you that he didn't want a relationship? It doesn't make any sense, Rana," Laura said, rearranging loaves to fill in the gaps of what we had sold already.

"Dude, I know. My sister kinda said the same thing. I don't know," I replied, baffled.

"I mean, what did he say *exactly*?" she pushed.

I thought about it for a second, "He said it had to do with the fact that he lived here and I live out there... Something like that," I tried to recall.

"Ohhhhh. So, he doesn't want to do the long-distance thing, ya think?"

"Maybe. I mean I know he loves his job and his students... and I can't have my career here. Not until my fashion line is making a huge profit and even then..."

In Los Angeles, I had fallen into working in wardrobe departments for movies and TV. When I was still in fashion school I took an internship in L.A. to help on an indie film, and I had been working in the business ever since. But my real dream was to have my own women's line, something I was working hard to pursue every day. Laura was even letting me design her wedding gown.

Ryan was a first-grade teacher. And given how sweet he had always been with his younger sisters, I'm sure he was great at it. His patience made him a natural. And having a passion for helping children just made him even more attractive. I'm sure all the women teachers went crazy for him.

"I can kind of understand his position, long distance can be hard," Laura reasoned.

"I know, but, Ryan started texting *me*. Calling *me*. Day after day. I wouldn't have seen him again if he wasn't so persistent. He knew I didn't live in Cleveland and he never backed off. Talk about mixed signals."

I needed a break. "I'm going to get some lunch. I'll grab you a sandwich too."

But I still couldn't stop thinking about Ryan. Why would he reach out to me only to say that he didn't want anything serious? What kind of weird game was he trying to play here?

FALL OF 1996, 8TH GRADE
#CaughtRedHanded

"But won't your mom be coming home soon?" I whispered into the phone.

"No. She went shopping with my sisters. That's going to take at least like, five hours. I mean, you're a girl, you know how long something like that takes."

I must admit, Ryan had a point. Shopping is something women generally don't want to rush.

I had broken up with Anthony shortly after Mary's party. He was always pulling me away from my friends and I had had enough. Not to mention, he didn't have a clue about how to treat a girl with respect. I was done. Plus, it was our last year at Munson and I didn't want to be tied down to someone who wasn't in our clique.

When Ryan got wind of the break-up, he called to see how I was doing. He even offered to call Anthony himself when Anthony kept pestering me to get back together.

Ryan was opportunistic. He just happened to be there when I needed him, and this time he wasn't backing down. And I knew almost immediately that I wanted to get back together with him. He was a nice change from Anthony who was, as my friends described, 'sooo into himself.'

Ryan told me all the things every girl wants to hear: how he couldn't stop thinking about me, how he never stopped loving me, and how he never would. I knew that we had to be together. If we didn't, I would have been fighting the inevitable. Ryan and Rana together again, was the common chant among our friends. Could we make it last this time? No pressure.

"Well, OK. Maybe" I replied, playing hard to get. I didn't really want to say no, but I needed to be convinced. Hey, I loved the thrill of living on the edge as much as anyone, but getting caught fooling around by parents wasn't my idea of fun.

"Come on, I'm dying to see you. This may be our only chance for you to be here without anyone else around—to be in my bedroom with the door shut."

Whoa. Did he just say that? I had to admit I was thinking it, but...being in a boy's bedroom with the door shut was something I had to be prepared for. I mean, I had done 'things' with boys before. Making out, yes, even second base, but I hadn't been to a boy's house when his parents weren't home. Ever. That meant that anything could happen, and it scared me a little.

"Yeah, with the door shut..." I said apprehensively.

Ryan could sense I was nervous.

"Hey, don't you trust me? I would never do anything to make you uncomfortable. We...could watch a movie if you want. My dad just bought me *Billy Madison*."

I giggled. He always knew how to make me feel better. That's Ryan Cavanaugh.

"I trust you. I'll leave in ten minutes," I said giving in. I couldn't say no to him. And, I had to admit, I was a little excited.

"Yes! Awesome, baby I'll see you then."

I smiled as I started playing with a loose thread I had found on my pillow.

"Rana?" he asked making sure I was still on the line.

"Yeah? I'm here."

"I love you honey. You're my everything."

I tried to hide my smirk as if he could see it on the other end of the phone.

"Aww. I love you too," I responded. It was only right to say it back. Besides, I had very strong feelings for Ryan. And, at the time, those feelings were probably the closest thing I felt to actual love.

It wasn't the first time we said those words. Heck, Ryan said them to me when we were in the fifth grade. And several times since we got back together.

But still, those words, 'I love you,' made me nervous. Ryan was always so sure of himself and the things he declared. But I wasn't.

"Good. Now get over here, I wanna kiss you."

"Are you going to walk or do you need a ride?" my mom asked after I told her I was going over to Ryan's.

My mom was always very laid back about the things I did. At times, I felt like she didn't care what I did at all. But, looking back, maybe she just trusted me a little too much.

"I'll just walk," I replied.

"His parents are going to be there, right?" my dad chimed in from the other room.

There it was, the question I was trying to avoid. Leave it to my dad. He could smell mischief ten miles away.

He obviously wasn't watching the football game as intently as I thought. I swear he hears everything in this house.

"Yes Dad, it's a Saturday morning," I said, rolling my eyes as if I believed my own lie. I hated lying to my dad, but this time I really didn't feel that guilty. It was like going to be with Ryan was something that I was meant to do. Ryan and I were back together and I found myself not caring about anything else. Everything was right in the world.

"All right, just be home in a couple of hours. You don't need to be at some boy's house all day, even if that boy is Ryan Cavanaugh" my dad answered back.

"He's my boyfriend and I've known him since— "

"Yeah, yeah, I'm not interested, Rana. Just be home soon," he interrupted.

"Fine." I sulked. I grabbed my purse and jacket and headed out the door.

"Hey, where's she going? I thought she had to do chores this weekend," Antonia whined. I hadn't noticed her sitting on the couch next to my dad. She ripped off her headphones and stopped her CD player as she gave me a smirk.

I shot her an evil look. My parents obviously forgot that earlier in the week Antonia and I had been punished with extra chores. We always fought over the same thing--clothes. I had 'borrowed' her Doc Marten's without asking.

"Relax, Tonia. She can do them when she gets back. And tomorrow, right, Rana?" my mom asked, stirring her tomato sauce. She started her sauce in the mornings and let it simmer until suppertime.

"Yes." I sulked.

"She always wiggles her way out of stuff, Mom. It's not fair!"

I ran out the door before they could change their mind.

On the walk, I dug through my purse: gum? Check. My coin purse with the change from last weekend's movie? Check. I didn't need any money, but you never know- a girl needs to be prepared for anything. I rummaged some more: nail file, a friendship bracelet from Laura (there it was, I'd been looking for that), a pen, a mirror, my tiny pink phone book with all my friends phone numbers, in case I needed to contact them with an important question (after all, I wasn't sure where this would all lead), and, most importantly, my chap stick. Lip Smackers cherry flavor, of course. It was Ryan's favorite, and I would have died if I had left it at home. I applied a thick layer.

"OK, I can do this," I thought, feeling a little more confident.

As I approached Ryan's blue saltbox house, I got butterflies. We had kissed. We had even French kissed at the mall one day, but we had never been in a house without parents before now. I had only been in his room two times before.

Once was after a football game last week while his parents, brother and two little sisters were home. Much to Ryan's dismay, Molly and Michelle were in his room with us practically the entire time, asking me questions like, "So, when I'm big I'll get to be a cheerleader with pom-poms, too?"

The other time was last year when his mom asked if I could baby-sit one of his little sisters for a few hours. As I chased Molly around the house, I wandered off into Ryan's room. In some ways, it was a lot like a thirteen-year-old boy's room might look. Sports memorabilia everywhere, a poster of Michael Jordan's wing-span, and a pile of *Thrasher* and *Sports Illustrated* magazines. But Ryan wasn't your average teenage boy, and upon closer inspection, something was different. He was meticulous about the way things looked, especially himself. Because his mom was a makeup artist, bottles of expensive cologne and hair products were neatly arranged on his dresser. Combs of all shapes and sizes sat next to them. His hair was just like everyone else in his family, shiny and thick. The way he styled it reminded me of Brandon from my favorite show, *Beverly Hills 90210.* He kept his shoes very clean (even his cleats) and to no surprise, in two tidy rows in his small closet.

After thinking about whether I should knock or ring the door-bell, I decided that knocking would be more mysterious. As I wait-ed, I heard him yell something that resembled 'I'm coming,' and I anxiously stared at the door knocker in front of me.

He swung the door open with a sideways smirk on his face.

"You made it. I thought you'd never get here," he said out of breath as he looped his pointer finger into mine and gently pulled me through the door.

"So, my room's over there, if you want to see it again," he said slyly. He had just showed me the new Super Nintendo and Easton base-ball bat he received for his birthday.

"No little sisters to interrupt us or anything like that," he said as he stopped me in the hallway and kissed me. Caught off guard, I gave in and let his warm lips press against mine. He opened his mouth and I followed suit.

We eventually made it to his room. I couldn't believe I was ac-tually on his bed, making out! I was feeling so many things at once. Excitement. Panic. Confusion.

I pulled away and sat up to catch my breath. I'm going to call Laura as soon as I get home and tell her every detail about this, I thought.

"Whoa," was all I could muster.

"What? Are you OK?" Ryan said.

"Yeah. Fine. Are, are you?"

"I'm good. Perfect. I don't want this to end," he said as he leaned in and gave me a peck on the lips. He seemed like such a pro at this even though neither of us had much practice.

"I knooooow. This is great. Are we going too fast?" I asked.

"What? Which part? Did I go too far when I went up your shirt?" Ryan asked hoping he didn't cross a line. Hoping more that I enjoyed it as much as he did.

I giggled. "No, it's fine, I just...I don't know. I just need to take a break for a minute."

"Right," Ryan said sitting up. We both stared at the blanket we were laying on. It had the Chicago Bulls logo on it. "So, are you glad you came over?"

"Definitely," I paused. "But, I'm kinda scared your mom's gonna come home. We'd get in so much trouble."

"Rana, she's not coming home soon, you can relax," Ryan said as he laid his mouth on mine. I fell into his arms and let myself relax into the moment.

The next fifteen minutes were dreamy. Suddenly, we both jolted up as we heard something outside. Looking out the window, we saw Ryan's mom and dad getting out of the car with his sisters and brother.

"Uh...OK- quick! Get in the bathroom!" Ryan said, panicked, as we both scrabbled off his bed. He threw my purse and shoes at me.

"Ohmygosh, Ryan!" I said, horrified but following orders.

"I know, I'm sorry!" he said, rushing me into the bathroom that connected to his room and shutting the door behind me.

I could hear him fidgeting with his comforter; probably to make sure it didn't look like two people had just made out all over it. He then scampered out the door.

I sat on the bathroom floor, my heart pounding.

I knew something like this would happen, I thought, afraid and exasperated all at once. Why did I listen to him? Shopping doesn't take five hours, what was I thinking?!

I could hear talking. This. Was. Not. Happening!

A few moments later Ryan's bedroom door opened. I froze, listening as the footsteps got closer. Was it Ryan? I cradled my knees and squeezed my eyes shut as the door swung open, praying I wasn't about to see his mom glaring down at me.

"Hey Rana," Ryan's brother, Jason said chuckling as he looked down to see me practically curled up in the fetal position.

"Jason! What...did you know I was in here?"

"Yep, I ran into Ryan in the garage. He filled me in," he said amused.

"Are you going to help get me out of here?" I whispered.

"Yes. Here's the plan. You're going to come through the hall-way— "

"What?! The hallway?! But — "

"Shhh! Listen, just trust me."

Sure, that's what your younger brother just said an hour ago, and now I'm shacked up in a bathroom clenching my purse. What is it with these Cavanaugh boys and trust?

"Fine," I said sighing. "What's the plan?"

"Just follow my lead, I've snuck girls outta here once or twice before," Jason said with the same sideways smile his brother had.

I laughed nervously, partially because an older boy was talking to me.

I grabbed my purse as I quietly followed Jason through Ryan's room. When we approached the hallway, we began tiptoeing. He looked back at me with his pointer finger to his lips. Duh. Didn't he realize I knew to be quiet?

Jason peeked around the corner into their living room. There was Ryan, getting the full run down from his mom about the shopping trip. Molly and Michelle occasionally chimed in with their two cents, while their dad channel surfed on the couch.

As we slinked past, I smiled as I caught a glance of Ryan with his sisters. There he was parked on the carpet, looking excited as Michelle showed off her new dress. He really was playing this off perfectly.

We walked right through the kitchen to the front door. Almost free! Jason slowly unlocked the deadbolt but the click seemed thunderous. We both tensed up for a second. Had somebody heard? No change. The conversation in the living room continued like normal, we both looked at one another in relief. He opened the front door for me and I slipped through. I turned and shot him a wave goodbye as he softly closed the door behind me.

So much for trusting Ryan.

I ran home as fast as I could trying to hold back the tears. When I got there, I raced upstairs to my room, not stopping to say anything to my family who were still in the living room. No one seemed to notice. I threw myself on my bed and into my pillow. That was mortifying, and it could have been so much worse.

Ryan called me later to apologize. I listened as he told me a million times how sorry he was and how he swore he wouldn't tell anyone at school. He promised he really thought his parents were gone for the rest of the afternoon.

"So, you want to watch Saturday Night Live with me?"

"Yeah right, like I could come over so late," I said.

"No, I mean, together on the phone. Just you and me. It'll be hilarious. I heard Dr. Dre's gonna be on tonight," Ryan said trying to persuade me.

I started to soften.

"You mean we just sit here on the phone all night and watch at the same time?"

"Yeah, or until our parents kick us off the phone," he said.

"Okay. Call me at eleven?" I replied.

"It's a date."

And just like that, my frustration and embarrassment started to go away. Only Ryan could win me back so quickly, I should have known I couldn't stay angry at him for long.

♥ GROWN UP US – DECEMBER 24, 2008 ♥
#GuyCode

"I just don't get it, man. I ticked her off or something. She won't text me back and I texted her like four times today," I vented.

"Whoa, four times? You better cool it. You can't give her the power like that, bro," Jason replied. We were grabbing lunch after doing the last of our holiday shopping.

"What do you mean 'power?'"

"What I mean is that you can't keep texting her and putting the ball in her court. You text once *maybe* twice and if she doesn't get back to you then you wait. For however long it takes."

"I'm not going to wait, if I want to talk to her then I'm going to send her a message," I said. "Besides, that's ridiculous. Rana doesn't play games."

"Are we talking about the Rana from when we were kids?"

"Yeah. Why?"

"Dang, how'd you end up with her again? I haven't heard her name in a while."

"It started a month ago, around Thanksgiving, but it's a long story," I answered.

"All I know is that every chick plays games, don't be naive. They're weird. And crazy. Yeah, weird and crazy is a good description," Jason said shoving fries into his mouth.

"I guess. I mean, I even went to Starbucks and got her a coffee. I brought it back to her while she was still in bed. Name a guy who does that?"

Jason looked at Ryan in disbelief. He was sometimes amazed at how different they were, despite being brothers. Since they were kids, Jason had tried to teach Ryan about women and the rules of dating. But he never wanted to listen "Pfft, not me." Jason said taking another bite.

Having been married for several years and now with three young kids, he found it pointless to try so hard to be romantic. "I'll give it to ya, though. You were workin' it. And you didn't even have to 'cause you already got the goods," he chuckled.

"Nah man, it's not like that," I shook my head. I didn't bother explaining things like this to Jason. He would believe what he wanted to believe. Like a lot of married men, he lived vicariously through his bachelor friends. "But I just don't get why she's blowing me off," I marveled.

"What'd you guys talk about this morning? Something had to have pissed her off. A girl just doesn't give you the silent treatment for no reason. Trust me, you screwed up."

I gave it some thought as I took a long sip of iced tea. "Well, I told her I wasn't looking for a relationship, but, she said she felt the same way."

"Dude! You slept with her last night— "

"We didn't sleep together, Jase. We just kissed."

"Yeah, sure. Whatever," he shoved more fries into his mouth, "you do all of that and the next morning you tell her that you don't want anything more from her and you're wondering why she's mad? You crack me up," he quipped, his voice muffled.

"What, you think that's it? Like I said, she agreed with me. I mean, she doesn't even live here, she's not looking at me as a serious boyfriend, especially one who lives across the country."

"And she said that? Like you heard her say those exact words? Or did she just say, 'yeah, sure'?"

"OK, I'm starting to see your point. She also did seem to hesitate before answering me."

I threw my hands up.

"Uh-huh. That's why she's pissed," he said stuffing the rest of his chicken sandwich in his mouth. "So, tell me, what's April going to say about last night?" he asked.

I stared at my untouched food, "She doesn't know and I'd like to keep it that way."

April was out of town visiting her parents in D.C. for Christmas, so Rana stopping by last night came with zero risk.

"Playing the field?! You dirty dog, you," nudged Jason.

"No, it's not what you think. I mean, I... She's not really..."

"What?"

"Well with Rana— "

Jason reached for the vibrating phone in his pocket, "Shoot, it's the wifey. I gotta get this," he said getting up from the table.

I sipped my drink. Could Jason be right? Did Rana just agree to placate me? Could she really want to get serious?

I checked my phone for any messages. Still no text from Rana. Two from April.

DECEMBER OF 1996, 8TH GRADE
#Ouch

"I know the Christmas dance is in two days, but I've gotta do this." I said.

"I mean, that's like the cruelest thing you can do, Rana," Laura replied, frustrated.

"Well, I don't know, I just want to be free. Free to dance with whoever I want and free to talk to whoever I want. You know, he got bent outta shape the other day because Eddie and I were *talking* in science class? He calls me like five times a day to talk about God knows what and he's getting super clingy. I can't take it anymore!" I pleaded my case.

Things with Ryan hadn't been going well for the past few weeks. I was starting to get that itch to be free—spend more time with my girlfriends (without the guilt) and perhaps play the field a little. I was starting to notice some of the other guys in our grade, like Eddie.

But also, Ryan's dad was up for a big promotion at work that would take the family out of state. He promised it would have no effect on our relationship but I wasn't so sure. As much as I hated to admit it, I was the jealous type and the mere thought of him being so far away without me knowing who was at his new school, what his friends were like...I thought I'd better end it before it gets to that.

"Yeah, well, maybe it's because Eddie has the hots for you in a major way. And he tries to flirt with you all the time, Rana. And you know it!" Laura retorted.

I could sense her judgement. I sighed as I sat and thought about it for a minute. Eddie and I had been good friends since we met last year in health class. We immediately hit it off, mainly because he could make me laugh. Heck, he made everyone laugh. He was our unofficial class clown.

I decided Laura was right. "Well, maybe I want to flirt back. And not just with Eddie but with— "

"Anthony?" Laura said cutting me off.

"Yeah! Maybe Anthony, is that such a crime, Laura? That I want to have a life outside of Ryan? Why do you always make me feel like I'm a criminal or something? I'm not cheating on him or anything, I want to break it off way before anything like that happens!"

Anthony still called me, despite my relationship with Ryan. I knew it was wrong to take the calls but I didn't have the heart not to. Plus, it was so out of character for him to be vulnerable and hint that he wasn't yet over me. Occasionally running into each other on Friday nights at the skating rink only fueled the fire.

Skate nights were quickly becoming my friends' favorite activity on the weekends. It was where most of our flirtatious interactions with boys took place. The occasional French kiss, too.

Laura and I both got quiet as we sat on the gymnasium bleachers waiting for cheerleading to start.

"Look, will you just give him the note tomorrow?" I said turning to her.

She looked at me then down at the note.

"Fine. I'll do your dirty work," Laura said giving in and shoving the note in her backpack.

"Thanks, Lor, I owe ya one," I said bumping her knee with mine.

"Yeah, yeah. Let's warm up before coach gets here."

As practice started, I had an uneasy feeling. Was I making the right choice? Was this going to be something I regretted like last time?

I didn't sleep a wink that night.

"Well?" I said to Laura as she approached me the next morning in the hallway. She sighed.

"I tried giving it to him in language arts."

"What? What do you mean 'tried?'" I asked baffled.

"He already knew what the note said. He handed it back to me without even reading it," Laura gave the note back to me. It was still folded up, clearly nobody had read it.

I was speechless."He was pretty upset."

"Really? Like upset how?" I asked not sure if I could bear to hear the answer or not.

"Like, he was choked up," Laura said softly.

"What? Are you sure?" My voice got quieter.

She shot me a look that implied she wouldn't joke about something like this.

Suddenly, Ryan turned the corner and our eyes met. He quickly looked away and I felt like everything was moving in slow motion. That simple act pierced through me like a knife. The pain worsened as he approached a group of our friends that included Natasha, giving everyone high fives like they were going out of style. I watched closely as he and Natasha exchanged playful banter. Now, he was all smiles like none of this fazed him whatsoever.

Laura looked at me, then back at him, then back at me again. "Uh, Rana?"

"What?" I said not breaking my gaze.

Laura tipped her head towards Ryan.

Ryan chatted with the guys for a minute, until Eddie suddenly grabbed his arm and handed him a note. Was that *the* note?

On a three-way call last night between Holly, Laura and I, Holly told us that she heard from Ben that there was a rift between Eddie and Ryan. And we all had a hunch that it was because of me. Ben had told Holly that an argument had started between Eddie and Ryan when they were playing football in Ryan's back yard this past weekend. And that even Ryan's older brother, Jason got involved.

It was no secret Eddie had a crush on me, and I suppose I enjoyed the attention. I assumed that Ryan didn't know that Eddie had asked me out at the skating rink a few weeks ago. He was Ryan's friend so his constant flirtation was something that upset Ryan, much like Natasha's annoyed me.

Now there was a note floating around and we were dying to get our hands on it.

"I'm just sick and tired of not talking to you about sports etc. I'm not gonna let rana break up our friendship, because we were just fighting over her. I'm sorry for being such a dick to you at my house and I hope we can be friends. Ryan W/B."

"Ryan, First off I agree with you about Rana (she's being the biggest bitch). But it wasn't even you that I was really mad at it was your brother. But as far as me and you well we'll just have to see what happens."

I highly doubt I was being 'the biggest bitch.' Surely there were bigger bitches out there.

Now, Ryan was walking back in my direction. Oh God, was he going to say something to me?

Instead, he walked right past me without so much as even looking in my direction. I couldn't stop staring at him as he headed down the hall until I lost sight of him in the swarm of kids rushing to their next class. I winced when I realized I may have just lost him altogether.

Eddie sat next to me in Social Studies class. He leaned over in the middle of Miss Middleburg's lecture: "Hey, I heard the news," he said grinning.

I looked over out of the corner of my eye. "Yeah," I responded. I wasn't ready for the full court press, which I suspected was coming. Besides, it was the only thing I could whisper without the whole class hearing- especially Miss Middleburg.

"Yeah, well...come on, go to the mall with me sometime?"

I squirmed in my chair a bit. What should I say? I was kind of interested, but I didn't want to hurt anyone's feelings, especially Ryan's. This felt too soon.

Avoiding the question, I looked around and spotted Natasha. I watched as she pretended to be *so* interested in the Cold War. Wasn't she just little Miss Student of the Year? What a phony.

Again and again she tossed her perfectly straight, blonde hair around. She was nothing like me and perhaps this was part of why I felt so threatened by her. She had fair skin and faint freckles; I was olive toned with the occasional blemish. Natasha was as thin and frail as they come; I was fit and curvy. She had blue eyes; I had green. Was she Ryan's type? Or was I?

She reapplied her glittery chap stick for about the hundredth time that period. I bet she was just thrilled to hear that Ryan was back on the market. Probably even more thrilled than Eddie.

I looked back at Eddie who was still waiting for my answer. "Uh, sure, what the heck."

"Just because we broke up doesn't mean we can't have a good time," I reminded Ryan as we entered the decorated gymnasium.

"Yeah, I know. You told me that already," he grunted.

"OK, I just...I want you to have a lot of fun tonight. Save a dance for me?"

Before he could answer, the swarm of friends who were anxious to greet us interrupted. As Laura and Holly were gushing about how good the DJ was, I glanced over at Ryan to see him slapping hands with his basketball teammates. He was then whisked away to the punch table. Natasha and her new sidekick, Julie, were also there.

"They're playing Black Street!" Laura gasped.

"Come on, we gotta go dance!" screeched Holly. My friends carried me with them to the dance floor.

"Look at that slut!" Laura shrieked, nodding towards Natasha.

Sure enough, Natasha was slowly making her way to Ryan.

"Yeah, I saw that one coming!" I yelled back above the music.

We watched in awe as Natasha stroked Ryan's arm and giggled at every word he and his friends said. She probably didn't even understand all the inside jokes they were telling.

"Do you care?" shouted Holly.

"Nope! Not tonight!" I shouted back. I was enjoying this moment with my friends—I didn't need or want any of the drama.

With Christmas break coming, I had a lot to look forward to. Why should I let my break up with Ryan ruin my night?

"Hey! Whaddya say, will you dance with me?" Eddie asked loudly approaching our circle.

I blushed at his directness.

"Thanks, but I'm dancing with the girls right now. Maybe later," I hollered back.

"All right, you better save a dance for me!" Eddie barked right before joining our other friends on the dance floor.

I really wanted to dance with Eddie, but despite everything I had just been thinking about, I was just still a little nervous to hurt Ryan's feelings more than I already had. Ryan had made it clear that he wasn't on board with the breakup. He had asked what he could do to fix things. The truth is, there was nothing he could do. I just wanted to be free. I had come to envy my girlfriends who only had to worry about their nail polish and history homework, without the added distraction of a relationship.

I glanced at Ryan who looked away quickly. How long had he been staring at me?

As the night wore on, Ryan and his friends finally joined us on the dance floor. It was getting very hot and stuffy in the gymnasium, so much so that the guys were unbuttoning the tops of their dress shirts and loosening their ties. My plaid wool skirt and red sweater were equally unforgiving.

At the dance, throwing up the ever popular, 'west side' sign (some
of us better than others). And an outfit is never complete without
a scrunchie around your wrist.

As we danced, sweat poured off us, hormones were flying, and
bodies were brushing up against each other, moving rhythmically to
everything from the Spice Girls, to Bush, to TLC. It was a great time.

Suddenly, all my friends paired up, dancing to the sultry beats of
Keith Sweat's new song. Only Ryan and I were conveniently without partners. Why did it always seem to happen this way: Ryan and
Rana. Alone. Where were Eddie and Natasha when we needed
them?

Fearless as usual, Ryan walked over and placed both hands on
my waist. He slinked behind me and began to sway back and forth

to the music. His body got closer to me with each movement. What made him think he could just grab me and do as he pleased? And why wasn't I stopping him?

"So...I guess I saved a dance for ya," he whispered in my ear.

Fate was a funny thing.

"You did...thanks," I replied hoping he could hear me.

"So, are you having a good time?" he asked.

"Yeah. Definitely. You?" I projected back.

"Yeah, for sure. Can I ask you something, Rana?"

I nodded. In this moment, I would hang on to his every word.

"Do you mind if I ask Natasha out?"

Whoa, what? My heart sank and my hips stopped moving. This is not what I was expecting.

"Does it bother you? I mean, is it too soon?" Ryan asked quietly, into my ear. He must be reading my body language.

I turned around. "Uh, no. No, it's not," I sputtered.

"OK. Cool. I just wanted to make sure you heard it from me first, ya know?"

"Right. Um thanks," I said pretending I wasn't upset. I turned back and continued dancing.

I'm OK. This is a good thing, Rana. He's moving on and now you can too. You're hanging out with Eddie soon and that's something to be excited for, right?

I could see Laura and Holly dancing with their respective partners. They looked so happy. That would be me again soon.

♥ GROWN UP US – CHRISTMAS EVE, 2008 ♥
#GiveMeStrength

I didn't really have time to be depressed. It was Christmas. And I love Christmas. I'd been very eager to spend it with my family. Since moving to Los Angeles, I didn't get to see everyone as much as I wanted. I was determined to enjoy the holiday—not spend all my time thinking about Ryan.

I hopped in the shower to wash the market off, replaying this morning's conversation over and over again in my head. You shouldn't have gotten so attached, I told myself as I let the sweltering water flow over my face.

I turned off the water and reached for my towel. As I dried my hair, I gave myself a pep talk in the mirror:

"This is going to be great. Tonight is going to be really fun. You can still pull yourself together and have a good time."

I applied my make-up and threw my hair up in a bun. I put on the chunky green sweater my mom got me a few years back. Would anyone remember I wore it last Christmas?

Who am I kidding, I don't even care.

I got ready in my parents' bathroom instead of the one I grew up using. I just liked the feeling of being in my dad's space.

Coming home always made me feel closer to him—as I got ready, I liked thinking about what he might be saying to me in this very moment.

He never would have gone for this; he would have complained that my hair was getting everywhere and then kicked me out for being messy. Eventually, I would have done what he said, but later he would have let me know he was sorry by poking fun at me until I laughed.

My mom on the other hand, didn't mind a bit. She preferred her bathroom messy.

"It looks lived in," she would say.

After all those years of my father's compulsive cleaning habits, I think she was relieved to be able to live in disarray. At times, I had trouble holding my tongue about all the clutter. Once when I suggested she get a maid service, she accused me of being like my dad. She thought it was an insult, but I didn't.

I felt my phone buzz.

Another text... Ryan?

Hi. Merry Christmas! Coming soon??

It was just my cousin, Annabelle. My face fell in disappointment.

I sent back a polite, "Merry Christmas! Be there soon!" and took a final look in the mirror. On the outside I looked all right, but on the inside I was falling apart. Fake it 'til you make it, right? Maybe my feelings would eventually catch up to my outward appearance.

VALENTINE'S DAY 1997, 8TH GRADE
#LoveHurts

I loved choir. Our teacher, Mrs. Linnell, was so enthusiastic it was hard *not* to have fun. We all preferred it to our regular classes where we had to sit still at a desk. The choir room was in the basement of our school. It was lofty with tons of instruments scattered throughout and a grand piano, where Mrs. Linnell sat for every class. We sat on risers but had to stand whenever it was time to get serious and sing.

We were starting to learn the music for the annual Munson spring concert. This year's theme was Disney.

As we stood up and began to go over the soprano part for a *Beauty and the Beast* number, something caught my attention.

Laura was waving frantically through the glass in the classroom door. I couldn't tell what she was saying.

I pointed to myself, "You want me to come out there?" I mouthed pointing back to her. She nodded eagerly.

I looked at Mrs. Linnell who was seated at the piano perusing her sheet music for the alto part. "Um, excuse me, Mrs. Linnell?" I said raising my hand.

"Yes?" she said looking around for the face to go with the voice. "Yes, Rana?"

"Can I go to the bathroom?"

She sighed.

"OK, but please hurry back, we have a lot of work to get done."

I leapt off the riser and grabbed a hall pass from a hook on the wall and ran out the door.

"What is it Laura, are you trying to get me in trouble?!" I said softly. It was fun to be mischievous. We hardly ever were.

"Oh relax. I have a surprise for you. Well, *I* don't have a surprise for you but...someone else does," Laura said looking away.

"What? What do you mean? Laura, did Ryan put you up to something because I told him not to— "

"Listen: just go upstairs to where his locker is. I gotta get back to class. Bye!" Laura ran down the hall chuckling.

"I'm going to get you for this!" I yelled after her.

I didn't like when Laura and Ryan conspired behind my back. Ever since he had broken up with Natasha a few weeks ago, he had been hinting that he wanted me back.

I should have never told him the dirt I had on Natasha in the first place. I knew I was sending him the wrong signal, like I wanted to get back together. But I couldn't help it, I didn't like seeing them together.

Truth is, I didn't care if she stole a shirt from the mall and then gave it to Ryan. But I knew *he* would. Plus, that's what friends do- they tell each other stuff. It just became another reason for her to dislike me, but whatever, at least Ryan knew who she really was.

A month ago, I had met Jack, Laura's older next-door neighbor who went to a nearby Catholic high school. I had developed a serious crush on him and he was all I could think about. He wasn't the most handsome guy in the world, but he was so mysterious. He was quiet, but in a confident way—like he always knew what was going on around him but didn't need to waste his time talking about it. All my friends asked me what I saw in him and the truth was, I wasn't sure. I just knew I wanted to figure him out.

As I walked up the stairs to where Ryan's locker was, I saw him standing there in his neatly pressed, un-tucked polo shirt and light denim baggy jeans. His hands were in his pockets and his hair gel made his head glimmer underneath the hall lights. He cocked to the side as he watched me walk down the hall.

"You look good," he said as I approached him.

Classic Ryan- never afraid to make it clear what he wants. "Uh, thanks, Ryan. So do you." I meant it too.

"Rana, I'll get straight to the point," he said taking a deep breath. "You know I never stopped loving you, right?"

Oh gosh, here it comes, could I stay strong? I gave a slight nod as I bit my lip.

"Ryan, stop— "

"Wait. Just let me finish. Even when I was with Natasha, I didn't really want her. Well, I thought I did. But, I was just trying to forget you. And then you came through for me and told me who Natasha really was. You've always been a good friend to me."

He continued. "I want to be with you. Once and for all. Just you and me. No one else."

He got down on one knee. *No!*

Part of me wanted to run away—I couldn't hear this. I had moved on. But I knew I would always listen to every word Ryan had to say.

"Rana, please be my valentine?" Ryan said, smiling as he looked up at me.

I was stunned. I stared at him, speechless, not knowing what to say.

He stood up and opened his locker. "I got something for you." He handed me a box. "Open it. I thought you'd like it."

Still silent, I opened it to find a stuffed Eeyore. His thoughtfulness brought a smile to my face.

"Remember how you once said you felt bad for Eeyore? That everyone likes Pooh and the rest of them, but Eeyore... he's so sad all the time," he quipped.

I nodded. I couldn't believe he remembered that. I had said it months ago. And it was with our group of friends, I didn't realize anyone had even heard.

He looked at me, hopeful. I almost began to say what he wanted to hear, how thoughtful he was, how he knew me so well. But I couldn't. It was too late. I had to remain calm and speak the truth. That's what friends do.

"Ryan, I can't accept this," I started. "You're so nice. And you went through all this trouble... It's really sweet. But..."

I felt such pain for him. My stomach was twisting and turning like I was on a roller coaster. I was such a horrible human being!

"But you just can't be with me..." he said quietly. Now he was the one who looked away.

I hung my head down and nodded again.

He slammed his locker shut. "Ya know I don't get you, Rana. You act like the world is going to end when I tell you that I want to ask Natasha out, and then you tell me something that you know will break us up. I can't deal with this anymore. What do you want from me?"

He stared at me demanding an answer. But I couldn't muster one up. I handed Eeyore back to him.

"Just keep it. I don't want it. I don't want any of this," he said walking away in defeat. I watched as he stormed down the hall.

Why was I the one to blame? I told him not to do any of this. Was I supposed to lie to him?

And there it was: me, Eeyore, and a guilty conscience. Even when I was being honest I *still* managed to create a mess.

I started in the direction I came, but quickly made a detour for my locker. There was no way I could go back to choir with that much baggage.

♥ GROWN UP US – CHRISTMAS EVE, 2008 ♥
#BuonNatale

I put on a happy face even if it made me a liar. It was better than having to answer the million questions about why I looked so upset.

"Hi everyone!" I exclaimed above the roar as I walked in. We were at my grandparents' house for our annual Christmas Eve celebration—something not to be missed in an Italian family. It was usually one of my favorite times of year, and even now, it was comforting to see our extended family together. Wine was flowing as the aroma of pasta and seafood wafted through the air. The familiar sounds of my uncles arguing, my cousins laughing, and the younger grandkids digging through all the presents were welcome distractions. I didn't realize how much I needed this until I got there.

We were late (par for the course), and almost everyone seemed to have claimed their respective chairs for dinner at the huge dining room table. So, I made my rounds to each and every person with a kiss on the cheek, like a good Italian. It was part of my heritage and I embraced it. I greeted my Nonna first. Then my Nonno, and each of my aunts, uncles and cousins.

I had gotten used to spending the holidays without my siblings. Despite the amount of family that I had around, it still felt lonely without them. But Ohio is a long way from Florida and none of them (or their spouses) can tear themselves away from work this time of year.

It still amazed me that they all ended up down South. First, Joey after getting married. His wife wanted to be closer to her hometown. Then Antonia moved after Kevin was transferred through his company. Finally, Elisha and Stefan followed suit after Stefan's recent promotion. With my dad being gone, my mom talked about making the move herself.

I was glad they would all be making the trek to Joey's house to-morrow for Christmas Day, even if it was without me.

I made my way over to my twin cousins, Annabelle and Gia. At least they could come home for break. They were still finishing up college, Annabelle in Nashville and Gia in Chicago.

They knew that Ryan and I had recently reconnected. Or were having a fling. Or whatever I was calling this.

"Hey there, how are ya?" I asked Annabelle as we kissed on the cheek. She and her sister were seated at the smaller 'kid table' away from my aunts and uncles.

"I'm alright...how are you guys?" I said giving Gia a kiss.

Gia took a hard look at me, "What a liar!" she exclaimed.

I shushed her as we giggled. I did not need my news spreading around this crowd. Let's just say, the level of questioning would be intense.

"Seriously, is something up? I can sense these things," Gia asked as serious as a heart attack.

"You can 'sense these things?' What, now you're a psychic?" Annabelle sarcastically replied, the all too common dish in our fami-ly.

"I swear, you're gonna get it, 'Belle..." Gia laughed pouring her dressing on her salad.

Their banter was refreshing, familiar. It was cheering me up already.

I decided to get straight to the point.

"Well, Gia's right."

"Ha!" she said hitting Annabelle in the arm.

Annabelle glared at her, "Oh shut it, G." Gia smirked, pleased with herself.

"Tell me Ray, is this about Ryan or Jeremy?" she quizzed.

"Oh gosh, not Jeremy! If he knew anything about Ryan, I'd probably die," I said taking a sip of her ice water.

"All right, Mrs. Dramatic, so what's the problem with Ryan then?" she asked.

"Well, this morning Ryan told me he didn't want a relationship with me. So, there's that..." I said trailing off. They both knew that he meant a lot to me so I didn't have to explain any further.

"Whaaaaaa? That makes no sense," Gia assured me. Annabelle nodded in agreement.

"Right?! I mean you guys know everything that's been going on. But he must not *like me*, like me. He said so."

I had been keeping Gia and Annabelle in the loop mostly by way of Facebook. There was also the occasional phone call to help me analyze a text from Ryan. Plus, they were there the night Ryan and I 'ran into' each other. The night it all really began. Well, began again. So much had happened in one month.

Laughter erupted at the adult table and it distracted us as we tried to decipher what caused it. Our Zia Julia and Zia Maria were up in arms over something was all I could gather.

"Whoa, what did he say exactly?" asked Gia, turning the focus back to our conversation.

"Well, he told me that he wanted to make sure we were both on the same page and that he 'wasn't looking for anything serious right now,'" I said making air quotes with my fingers.

"Ohhh! Now maybe that doesn't mean..." Gia was trying to think of something that implied the opposite of what was already evident. "Like, what did you say after he said that?"

I gave her a look.

"Duh, I told him I felt that way too."

We all laughed at the craziness. They knew 'the rules' so it came as no surprise. But there was definitely something funny about a girl who lies her way through the beginning of a relationship to land the guy of her dreams. And he certainly was that.

And yes, we've all done it.

"Hang in there," said Annabelle. "I bet he'll come around."

"I'm not going to hold my breath," I said quickly. My phone vibrated in my jacket hanging on the back of my chair.

Are you avoiding me? Is everything cool?

"Shoot, it's Ryan. What do I say?"

Annabelle grabbed my phone to look at the text. "Sounds like he's worried he hasn't heard from you," she said with a slight smile. "At least let him know you're alive."

"This is throwing me for a loop. I need some time to think," I replied as I got up to go to the upstairs bathroom.

I needed to text him and tell him exactly how I felt. Screw the rules; I had to put it all out there in the open.

I tiptoed up the stairs and into the guest bathroom and sat on the toilet lid. No more games.

I began to type:

Yes, I'm avoiding you. Why wouldn't I?!

No, that's too much. I needed to stay calm. I didn't want him thinking I was mad. Or worse, that I'd been obsessing all day. Stop. Focus.

I erased the text and started over:

Sorry. I haven't been avoiding you. I just don't see the point in talking so much.

Ugh, that didn't sound right. ...I tried again:

Hi. Sorry I've been avoiding you. I guess I need some distance between us. I have a confession to make.

I took a big breath as I started to type the sentence that would make me totally vulnerable, throwing out everything I'd ever learned about relationships.

I'm starting to develop strong feelings for you and talking all the time isn't helping. If you don't want a relationship with me, I'm not sure I can handle a friendship with you.

I quickly hit 'SEND' before I could change my mind. What I wrote was the honest-to-God truth, and it was time to finally come clean. I exhaled loudly, I'd never felt so exposed. I was scared to death of what he was going to say. I stared at my phone imagining what Ryan was thinking as he read my text.

My phone vibrated- gosh, that was quick! I panicked as I saw his name pop up.

"Rana! Come and eat!" shouted my Nonna. I practically fell off the toilet as I snapped back to reality.

I caught my breath.

"Coming!" I yelled towards the door.

I stood up and looked at myself in the mirror. Should I open the message? What if Ryan was about to break my perforated heart? How could I possibly eat ravioli after that? I carefully considered waiting. But I didn't think I could keep up the brave face after reading Ryan's response.

I set my phone on the sink counter, and convinced myself I had said the right thing regardless of the outcome. No time for regrets even if I totally and utterly threw out the rulebook. That unopened text message would still be there after dessert. To make it that far, I'd have to leave the phone here so I wouldn't gawk at it during dinner.

I opened a drawer in the vanity and put my phone next to the tiny hotel soaps my grandparents collected from their many travels.

I turned off the light and closed the door behind me.

Nonsense. That's all this was, right?

I headed downstairs, knowing I was about to eat the fastest dinner I ever had in my life.

SPRING OF 1997, 8TH GRADE
#IPromise

"Well I don't suppose you want to sign my yearbook?" I asked Ryan.

"Why not?" he said exchanging the books in his hand for the ones on his locker's shelf. He kept his focus, never looking at me once.

"I don't know, I mean we definitely... had like, ups and downs this year. I guess. I would sign yours. I mean if you wanted me to," I replied.

He turned to me.

"Of course I'm gonna sign your yearbook. Hand it over," he demanded, holding out his hand.

I quickly gave it to him, and stood expectantly waiting for him to give me his.

"Oh, Craig Willoughby has mine. You'll have to get it from him at lunch or something," he said slamming his locker shut.

"Oh. Right. And when will you be done with mine because Holly said—"

He leaned in close to my face and whispered.

"You'll just have to wait and see." He brushed my shoulder lightly as he headed towards his class. His breath still tickled my ear, and a warm feeling rushed over my body. I felt as light as a feather.

Why did he always have to...mess me up? For a second, I thought he might kiss me. And I don't know if I would have stopped him. It's like we had this undeniable chemistry that came oozing out the second we were alone. I know it was always there, but it still surprised me when I felt it.

The warning bell rang and I began to move with urgency. It took me a few moments to realize I was headed in the wrong direction.

Damn you, Ryan...

The next morning, the girls and I were gathered around my locker. Holly was filling us in her Instant Message conversations with Ben lately. Laura and I were doing our best to confirm that her suspicions were right; he was definitely flirting.

"Here ya go, Rana- all done," Ryan said making his way through Holly and Laura, while looking me straight in the eye.

He plopped the yearbook in my arms and kept walking. I was caught off guard, but I finally managed, "Gee, thanks! That took like, forever!" Very smooth. He either ignored me or didn't hear me, but I had to take a stand in front of my friends.

Ryan headed towards Ben and Mike who were standing across the crowded hall.

Laura snatched the yearbook from me, "What's it say?!" she said opening it up.

"Laura, who cares? Just give it back," I huffed as I held out my hand.

"Oh. My. Gosh. He took up an entire page!" Laura screeched, showing Holly and Mary.

"Whoa, Rana, he totally did!" Holly chimed in.

"Like, wow, did you tell him he could do that?" asked Mary.

"Let me see!" I grabbed my yearbook back and there it was: lots of neat, cursive writing and his too-cool signature complete with his jersey number from basketball.

I skimmed over what he wrote before quickly shutting my yearbook, "The bell's about to ring, I'll look at it later," I said, knowing I needed time to read and analyze each word in detail.

"Oh, boo! We wanna see it now!" Laura hollered.

"Laura, I'll show you at lunch, now let's go to class!" I said hooking her arm into mine.

As we scurried along I looked back and spotted Ryan in the crowd. We locked eyes for a moment before I turned the corner. I hadn't told anyone that I spent most of last night wondering what he was writing.

Laura and I rushed into our home economics class just as the bell rang and took our assigned seats across the room from one another. I threw my books down and thumbed through the yearbook until I found Ryan's page. I spotted his cursive handwriting immediately and dove into his message, completely ignoring the day's lesson.

I read the message three times before I slammed the book shut— holy crap, Laura and the girls were gonna freak! I tried to turn my attention back to class, but I couldn't stop thinking about the promise that Ryan had written to me.

♥ GROWN UP US – CHRISTMAS EVE, 2008 ♥
#TextingWar

What did Ryan write to me? I couldn't get up the stairs fast enough. I threw open the door and yanked the vanity drawer open. My phone was lit up as if I had *just* received a text! I was so nervous, I almost dropped the phone in the sink as I went to open my texts.

There were two messages from Ryan. I braced myself as I sat on the toilet lid.

First, I re-read what I sent just to refresh my memory. It now sounded bolder than I had wanted it to be. Shoot.

I opened the first text:

Wow ok so we can't talk anymore?

Was that a rhetorical question? Did he even care? Could he be any more ambiguous? Hopefully the next text would shed some light on how he was truly feeling about all of this.

I opened the second message:

How would we have a relationship when you live in la and I live in cleveland?

More questions? Like I had all the answers. Or any, really.

Ryan was asking me about all the logistics, but I hadn't figured any of that out. I just knew in my heart I needed to be with him. I hadn't gotten too far beyond that. Was I asking for a long-distance relationship? Was that something *I* wanted? Could it work? I let out a big sigh. At least this wasn't a *complete* rejection...was it? Maybe Ryan was open to figuring it out.

Everything felt surreal, as I sat on the toilet and stared at my phone, I couldn't believe that I was back in the same place with Ryan Cavanaugh. Only this time we were adults. Time had passed, we both had experienced so much without each other and yet somehow here we were again—finding our way back to one anoth-er. How did this happen? It made me wonder how different things would be if I had never broken up with him in the sixth grade. Would we still be together now? All the questions had me reeling.

When I got downstairs, the focus had shifted from eating to pre-sents. My younger cousins were giddy as my Nonna passed out their gifts. As always, they were instructed to sit under the tree where they'd be in plain sight for us all to see.

Watching them open their presents was almost bittersweet. It was a little sad that I had outgrown that stage of life, but I was excit-ed for my little cousins who still got to experience it.

These days the 'big kids' were handed a Christmas card with a generous check inside, even my mom and the aunts got one. It was how my grandparents spread their wealth, and I always appreciated their thoughtfulness.

I took a seat on the couch next to my Nonno.

Nonno Tony was tall, slender and still very handsome despite being in his seventies.

Truly living the American dream, he had come from Italy and made a nice fortune starting the family landscaping business from scratch. My grandmother stayed plenty busy at home with their six children but still found time to paint. And she was a wonderful artist. Each one of us had been gifted at least one portrait of ourselves at some point in our lives.

I looked over at my Nonno; he was smiling at his great grandchildren while they ripped at the wrapping paper.

"Hey hun, have a seat," he said in his accented English. He spoke well, but there were still many phrases he carried over from the old country. I know he and Nonna still spoke in Italian to one another when they were alone.

My Nonno always called us girls 'hun,' and my Nonna called us 'shoog.' Which I assumed was short for honey and sugar.

"Thanks, Nonno."

"You feelin' OK? You seemed a little quiet during dinner. You and Annabelle and Gia weren't as loud like you usually are," he smiled.

To Italians, being loud only means two things: either you're angry or happy.

"Oh...yeah. No, I'm fine."

"Huh. All right then," he said.

We continued to make small talk. He asked if I was working on any new movies and what the actors were like. "He seems like a nice guy. Is he nice guy?"

As our conversation wrapped up, I spotted Annabelle and Gia by the drinks. I was dying to tell them about Ryan's texts to me.

"I'm going to grab Limoncello, Nonno, want some?"

"No, I've had too much," he patted his belly.

I casually strolled over to Annabelle and Gia who were pouring the Limoncello shots.

"Rana! Limoncello?" Gia said holding up a small glass.

"Definitely." A drink was just what I needed.

SEPTEMBER 1, 1997, 9ᵀᴴ GRADE
#PartyLikeIts1999

"Can I see the guest list?" mom asked.

"Ma, stop calling it that, it's just some of the people from school. Here," I said, planting it in her hand as I took a seat at the kitchen counter. I wanted to talk about the details of the fifteenth birthday party my parents were reluctantly letting me throw this evening.

She continued stirring her soup.

"Hmmm, ok," she said scanning the crumpled piece of paper.

We were two weeks into high school now but pretty much hung out with the same circle of friends, give or take a few. I'd been looking forward to this party since the end of the summer.

"What?" I said sensing that there was something more she wanted to say. I poured myself a glass of orange juice and breathed in the aroma of her famous chicken noodle soup—the smell was comforting. It was her ritual to make it when anyone in the house wasn't feeling well. Today, she was making it for Molly who was still recovering from tonsillitis.

"Nothing, I just noticed that your list is... numbered."

"So?"

"And you have a certain someone listed first. That's all," she replied.

"Let me see that," I said snatching it out of her hands. After examining the paper I immediately knew what she was talking about. How could I be so thoughtless?

"Huh. OK, so what's the big deal?" I said trying to downplay it.

"Nothing is a big deal. Just thought it was over between you two. So, is it?" she boldly asked. Her blonde hair and thin face were very different from mine. I got most of my looks from my dad: the dark hair, the athletic build, the defined jaw and the blue eyes. The rest of my siblings took after my mom. Not that any one of them could go wrong, they were both attractive people. My buddies even gave me a hard time about how good looking my mom was. But it was just to get under my skin.

"Yes. Definitely. We're just friends. Just like Natasha and me," I said changing the subject.

"I noticed she's been calling a lot lately," mom smiled.

"Yeah. She can be relentless," I laughed tasting a spoonful of soup she was offering.

"So, you're thinking of dating her again?"

"Well, I don't want a serious girlfriend. But she's liked me for a long time and like I said, she can be relentless. Needs more salt, Mom," I replied pointing to the spoon.

"I see your point, but is that a good enough reason to hang around someone?" she questioned.

"What do you mean?"

"I guess all I'm saying is make sure you're going out with her because you like who she is. Not because it's convenient," she said shaking more salt.

"Right. Yeah. I will," I sputtered.

She noticed the hesitation.

"If I remember correctly, there was something she did last year that didn't exactly thrill you."

I hadn't filled her in on any of the details of Natasha's shoplifting stunt but she knew when we suddenly broke up. And she knew that I'd been adamant about not getting back together despite the many phone calls Natasha made, trying to convince me to take her back. It was surprising how reluctant she had been to move on.

"I know Mom, but that was junior high. We're past that," I replied.

And I believed that. Natasha told me it was a stupid stunt. She had stolen that shirt for me because she wanted to give me a nice gift that she couldn't afford otherwise. She didn't have as much money as she let on, and her parents were in the middle of a nasty split. After getting some distance from the situation, I could see her point of view.

Natasha was always a little insecure and it was probably because the other girls never really accepted her. And in a way, Rana was to blame for that; whatever grudge she had for Natasha influenced the group. It was obvious Rana didn't like Natasha, especially when me and Natasha were dating. Why couldn't Rana get over it?

But that was getting into a whole other dimension of Girl World, and I knew better than to venture down that path.

"OK. I just hope you're right. Because Natasha wasn't even on your guest list," she said setting it down on the counter within arm's reach.

I rolled my eyes at the thought of her insisting on calling it a 'guest list' and picked up the paper again. My eyes went wide in bewilderment. Damn, how could I forget Natasha?

Ryan's Party List

* 1. Rana mancini
966 - 8736
(Y)   N

Date = Sept 1st
Time = 6-10 p.m.
Where = my place

Top of the 'Party List!'

OCTOBER 2, 1998, 10TH GRADE
#DATELESS

High School was different. My friends and I were surrounded by lots of unfamiliar faces, two hundred more to be exact. By the time we finished ninth grade, our tight knit group had somewhat disassembled. But not Laura and me; we stayed close, and being together on the cheerleading squad helped.

Ryan and I were simply friends. We didn't talk about getting back together and for the first time the pressure was off. I still felt our spark, and I'm sure he did too, but neither of us acted on it. For once, we seemed to be in a solid place and I didn't want anything to ruin that. Heck, I wondered if he even still remembered that promise he wrote in my yearbook two years ago.

High school left a lot to be desired when it came to my love life. But my active social life and cheerleading kept me busy. But being at all the football games and practices also forced me to be around Ryan a lot. We had both moved on, but, neither of us had entered into another serious relationship. That said, I was ready.

I had become fixated on Troy Palombo over summer break. He was a junior and on the football team, so I saw him frequently once school started. When I received a note in French class that he was into me too, I was ecstatic. After a few dates and some heavy make-out sessions in the front seat of his Eclipse, he quit paging me. The next day when I saw him at practice, he pretty much ignored me. I told the squad leader I felt sick, and spent the next two hours crying my eyes out in the bathroom. I tried to hide my devastation from my friends, but it was hard. This was the first time I had ever just been dropped—it wasn't something I was used to. Dating an upper classman clearly wasn't all that it was cracked up to be. I felt like a fool, but I had also learned my lesson.

The homecoming dance was in a few weeks, and all anyone was talking about was who was going with whom. After the fiasco with Troy, I wasn't ready to think about dating again, so I convinced a small group of girls on the cheerleading squad to go together instead of trying to find dates. But convincing the girls to stick together was easier said than done. One by one my girlfriends dropped like flies as they got asked to the dance. I was starting to get worried I would be going solo, since nobody seemed to be sticking to the plan. I had already turned down two boys myself, thinking we were still doing the group thing.

Not that I wanted to go with either of the guys who asked me anyways. One was Eddie. He still had a crush on me and claimed we had some unfinished business brewing from junior high. I couldn't disagree more; in high school, he had become quite the 'player.' It seemed he was with a different girl practically every week. Not something I was interested in pursuing.

The other was a boy named Ross Geller. He had the same name as the character from *Friends,* and that's all anyone ever talked about. He was also a junior but not very popular. The resemblance to the Ross Geller from the TV show was uncanny: tall, skinny, and geeky. He actually asked if I would 'be his Rachel.' Yeah right!

But who was left?

I'd been keeping an eye out for Ryan. It was only right that we accompany each other to our first high school dance. As friends, of course. But would he even ask me?

"Hmmm, let's see, what about anyone from the basketball team?"

"As if, Ma. It's football season. Like, that doesn't even make sense."

My dad laughed. Glad he could find the humor in all of this.

Antonia and I had been roped into helping my mom cook and clean for her monthly Saturday night card club.

"School dances are so lame. They're never as fun as they're cracked up to be," Antonia snarled. She was now a senior so my freshmen problems were at the top of her, that's-so-petty list.

I had finally let go of my idea to go with my girlfriends. They pretty much all had dates now, so I needed to figure out who was going to ask me—and fast.

"You know, I can ask Barb if Jonathan is going with anyone. They're coming tonight," my mom said.

"No! Ohmygosh, don't do that. I can't have you finding a date for me that is so embarrassing!" I said filling the candy dishes with Peanut M&M's as directed. I was quickly reminded why I kept my mouth shut most of the time.

"Yeah Ma, seriously," Antonia agreed.

"I don't understand how you have a problem getting a date, with how many boys call the house looking for you..." my mom replied, not in the least bit phased by my attack moments before.

My dad looked up from arranging the folding chairs he had just brought up from the basement.

"It doesn't matter. I don't even want to go. And it's a couple weeks away so, like, it doesn't even matter."

"You so want to go and you know it," Antonia gaffed. She rolled her eyes as she kept scrubbing crumbs of baked ziti out of the pan she was holding.

"Why are you even in this conversation?" I sneered.

She gave me a death stare in response.

It was Antonia's job to clean pots and pans and my job to clear the table and load the dishes. On the off chance that Elisha was home, her job was to set the table, a task I protested as too painless. My parents would say that she had loaded plenty of dishwashers when she was my age. I think they were just pleased she was sitting down with us to eat. I hated that she got the red-carpet treatment just because she came home from her stupid boyfriend's house.

"Well, have you thought about asking anyone? You *can* do that, you know," my mom replied as she motioned for me to get the tablecloths out for the card tables.

"No, Ma. It's not the Turn-Around-Dance, that's not until next semester," I said wishing she'd stop trying to find solutions.

"Fine then, what about the gown? All the time we spent on it, I want you to wear it."

My mom, grandmother and I had made my dress together. Fashion had started to become my obsession as of late. I even spent an entire weekend crafting all the cheerleading squad's hair bows for the Homecoming game.

But this dress was a masterpiece. I had designed the dress myself. It was peach colored with an open back. As master seamstresses, my mom and grandmother were more than happy to help. The thrill of wearing my one-of-a-kind dress was something I had been looking forward to. I had just assumed I would be either going with my girlfriends or with a date, not solo.

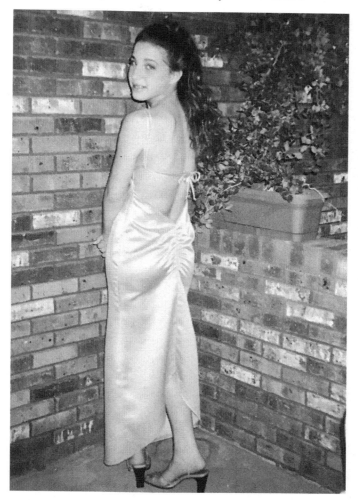

The infamous dress. Another one of my masterpieces...

I was just about to complain about how long the cleaning was taking when my mom blurted out, "Oh guess who I ran into yesterday at the mall? Ryan's mom! Did Ryan tell you? So, I guess they've already been looking at houses. Maybe that's why he hasn't asked you to the dance,because they'll be in Milwaukee. Antonia, don't put the ice in that, you have to use the ice bucket in the cabinet."

"Huh?"

"What?" she looked at me, bewildered.

"What do you mean 'Milwaukee?'"

"Ryan didn't tell you? They're moving."

♥ GROWN UP US – CHRISTMAS EVE, 2008 ♥
#TellItLikeItIs

Just breathe; you can type this...it was late and I was back at my mom's house. It had taken me awhile to think through how to respond to Ryan's recent texts. Maybe it was the long day, or one too many Limoncellos, but I finally decided I just needed to come clean—to throw out all the rules and tell Ryan what he needed to know.

All I know is that I want to be with you. IDK what else to sat

Crap! I mean:

Say. IDK what else to say not sat

Ohmygosh, Rana. You finally get the courage to say what you've been wanting to say for the last month and you have a major typo! Great.

OCTOBER 4, 1998, 10TH GRADE
#TheShoeIsOnTheOtherFoot

"Why didn't you tell me?" I demanded. No sense in trying to hide the fact that I was pissed. Ryan needed to know.

He avoided looking at me as he paid for the pencils he just bought at the school store.

"I want to know why I had to find out from *my mom*, Ryan. How could you keep this from me?"

He started walking down the hall, without acknowledging me. Was he hoping I'd go away like some pesky fly? The hall started to clear, as everyone began heading to homeroom.

"Ryan?" I said trying to catch up with him. "Ryan, stop!"

"What? What?!" he turned to me with frustration.

Startled, I gathered myself together.

"I want to know why you didn't— "

"Why I didn't tell you that I was moving to Milwaukee, right?"

I nodded.

"Because, I don't owe you anything, Rana. I hate how you think I belong to you and that you're so special, that you should be the first person I tell anything to. The truth is that you aren't."

"I never said— "

"You didn't say it but I know. I'm not your property, Rana. You're just...you're just some girl I used to date," his voice grew quieter as he said it.

We were the only ones left in the hall. The bell rang loudly to signal the start of homeroom. We were going to be late, but I didn't care.

I stared at Ryan in disbelief. Where was all this anger coming from? Why would he say those things? I thought we were friends. Wouldn't friends share something this important? If the shoe were on the other foot, Ryan would have been one of the first people I told. I assumed he valued our friendship in the same way. But clearly, he didn't. And it hurt like a bitch.

"Why are you looking at me like that? Did you think that I was over you or something? I wasn't, and you knew it. So, don't play dumb," he said conclusively, as if he had been waiting two years to tell me this. "Ya know, I'm actually glad we're moving because I need to start over. Ever since the fourth grade, this thing between you and me has been...exhausting. I just want it to be over."

I gulped as I tried to take it all in. Maybe Ryan and I were more different that I thought. I tried to think of something to say, some way to fix everything. But I could sense he was done talking.

"So... were you just going to leave without saying goodbye?" I muttered.

"Yeah. Probably..." he trailed off.

Ouch. The knot in my stomach tightened, and the lump in my throat was throbbing from holding back tears. I was about thirty seconds away from either crying or throwing up.

"OK...Well when do you go?" I managed.

"Tomorrow morning. I was on my way to the office to hand in my withdrawal papers," he said wrinkling them in his hands.

I thought Ryan and I had all the time in the world to be friends, or wherever else that might lead, if we decided to go down that road again. But that dream just burst—it was really over—he was moving like a million miles away.

"Oh. Right," I murmured.

His eyes grew soft as he finally looked at me. Even when he was trying to be a jerk, he doesn't really succeed.

"Can I at least have a hug?" I asked hesitantly.

I braced myself as he pulled me in, not knowing if it was because he really wanted to or if he just felt sorry for me. I suppose I didn't care. Inhaling his spicy cologne, I buried my head in his shoulder. His arms wrapped around me and he nuzzled my neck, his breath grazing my skin.

I tried to remember the last time I was in his arms but couldn't. This felt different. And wonderful. Kind of like... I was home.

I held him tight knowing that this moment could never happen again. And that I would probably want it to.

♥ GROWN UP US – CHRISTMAS DAY, 2008 ♥
#TheExFactor

I opened my eyes as the reality of what happened last night hit me like a ton of bricks. I never heard from Ryan after I sent that last vulnerable, gut-wrenchingly foolish text. I obsessed over it until I finally passed out.

I flopped out of bed trying not to think about the day ahead. My mom hosting Christmas Day came with a mountain of household tasks that I wasn't up for.

I slipped on thick socks and my hooded sweatshirt and took my phone off its charger. I noticed a text waiting to be opened. Ryan?

Hey. How's it going? Merry Christmas

"Oh crap," I grumbled.

Jeremy wasn't someone I wanted to think about right now. Although we had been broken up for almost five months, he was having a hard time accepting that the relationship was over. And it made me sick with guilt each time I had to remind him.

I kept telling myself that I didn't plan to hurt him. Sometimes people fall out of love—it's not like I could help it.

Jeremy and I had met in L.A. more than two years ago, at the Asian-fusion restaurant where he had just been promoted sous chef.

It was a favorite spot for me and some girlfriends. His light brown hair, dark eyes and freckles sprinkling his cheeks were irresistible, as was his charm.

He was a Southern boy who grew up in Louisiana and had moved to California a few months before we met to start his culinary career in a big city. His thick Southern drawl immediately caught my attention.

Apparently, he had his eye on me for quite some time but finally had the guts to introduce himself after sending over free desserts to our table. We quickly bonded over being newcomers to a big city. Jeremy would make me laugh as we'd talk about L.A. quirks, like how everyone wore the same uniform: jeans or sweats, how it took forever to drive anywhere, and how spastic his restaurant manager would get over celebrity clientele. We were just two small-town kids trying to navigate big ol' Los Angeles. I was the first real friend he made in L.A.

I should have known quickly that we weren't a good fit for one other. I mean, Jeremy was a down-home boy who loved to hunt and fish; I was an Italian fashion major who loved traveling. From an outsider's perspective, one might wonder what brought us together in the first place -a question I was asked almost immediately by multiple members of my outspoken family.

"Well we both moved to L.A., so we share a sense of adventure," I would reply, hoping they wouldn't pry any further.

And oddly enough, for a period of time I believed this was enough. I wanted to live my life audaciously, and I needed a partner who felt the same way. Jeremy seemed to fit the bill, and for two years it was fine.

Despite our differences, Jeremy seemed to appreciate who I was. He gladly met my family and soon preferred spending holidays with them in Ohio. Sure, he was a little taken back by how loud and rambunctious they could be, but could you blame him?

After a while I started to sense that he was running from his own roots. Almost like he wanted to forget about them all together. He was the only person in his family to leave their tiny town, let alone go to college. I always thought he had something to prove to the world and to himself.

A year into our relationship, he reluctantly agreed to bring me home for his father's retirement party. He was self-conscious about showing me the trailer that he grew up in and insisted we find a nice hotel in nearby Baton Rouge even though his mother made up their sofa bed.

Jeremy was the only child of two only children. In stark contrast to my family, holidays were only his parents and two grandparents. This didn't make his overbearing mother any easier to stomach. Even though Jeremy had left home for college, I was still to blame for 'keeping him in L.A.' Thankfully, Jeremy agreed that this idea was ridiculous.

"Just ignore her," he would tell me.

"Wouldn't it be easier if you corrected her?" I would respond, hoping to convince him to stand up to her.

But that was part of the problem: I was an outspoken Italian girl who needed to be with someone who had a strong voice, perhaps even stronger than mine. But that wasn't Jeremy; he could barely articulate how he felt about me. At first, this seemed stoic, mysterious, even coy. But eventually this translated to closed-off and emotionless.

Jeremy and I had only been dating for a couple of months the first time I thought about breaking it off. Deep down, I knew that we didn't have a future, but I was trying to ignore my instincts and give him a chance. I became a pro at rationalizing any negative thoughts away. Who cares if we'll never get married? I'm young and we're just having fun. We'll break up when it's time, besides, things could change. He could change. What I failed to realize was that I was wasting precious time with someone I knew I wouldn't marry. I should have been spending my first few years in L.A. enjoying being single and free of any attachments.

Two years in, I finally gained the courage to end it. In response, Jeremy miraculously felt brave enough to tell me how much I meant to him and how he'd be lost without me. But it was too late. I was ready to move on.

Jeremy didn't see it that way and clearly still felt like he could change my mind. Seeing him vulnerable and exposed was what I had been longing for all along. At first I was angry he didn't speak up sooner, but I got over it.

I deleted Jeremy's text. I was determined to make this Christmas a good one. I'd come all the way here and wasn't about to let a guy ruin that. Not Jeremy and not Ryan.

Auntie arrived early to help just like always. This was a welcome distraction and helped take some of the pressure off me.

I dragged tables and chairs up from downstairs while mom cooked and Auntie set the table. "Boy, it's sure cold outside. What is the weather like in Los Angeles?" Auntie asked. I really loved our talks. She was well-traveled and such an inspiration. Even at eighty years old, she was still going to Europe, Texas, you name it.

"Rana, go get ready," my mom said. "Everyone will be here in a half an hour and I don't want you upstairs primping." Auntie shot me a look indicating I'd better listen.

I darted upstairs and headed for the shower. I checked with my phone first. Nothing.

SUMMER OF 1999, GOING INTO JUNIOR YEAR
#MatchMakerMatchMakerMakeMeAMatch

"But I really want you to meet him, Rana," Antonia said. I was surprised she could still breathe while she lay intertwined with her boyfriend, Kevin in his backyard hammock.

They were the annoyingly affectionate couple who couldn't keep their hands off each other. I found it best to hang with them in groups so you had someone to talk to when they couldn't hold a conversation. But today it was just the three of us.

Kevin was from the wealthiest part of our town, and boy were his parents loaded, although no one was sure exactly how they came across their good fortune. Rumor had it his father was some sort of shady businessman, but none of us knew that for sure.

I was confused as to why we were still here. We were only supposed to grab Antonia's pager and head home. I was starting to feel like including me in this excursion was just Antonia's ploy to make sure our parents wouldn't be suspicious.

Just a few months earlier, I was deemed 'cool enough' for Antonia to 'let me' hang out with her, although she quickly lost patience if I started to act like an 'annoying little sister' (whatever that meant). In any case, spending time together helped remind her that our two-year age gap wasn't that big of a difference.

Ryan had been gone almost eight months. We hadn't spoken since I confronted him in the hallway the day before he left. I hoped he was doing okay in Milwaukee—some of our mutual friends shared that he was fitting in well. I also heard rumors that he was still in touch with Natasha, but I tried to ignore them.

"I don't know, Tonia. I kind of liking being single," I replied, getting tired of everyone thinking I needed to have a boyfriend just because they did.

Laura had had the same boyfriend since sophomore year, and I was constantly trying to skirt their set ups. I knew that my being single made me the dreaded third wheel. I'm sure she would have rather I had a boyfriend too so we could do the double-date thing, and she wouldn't have to feel guilty.

"Come on, Rana, please? You just have to promise me one thing."

"No I don't."

Ignoring me, she continued.

"No putting Bronson in the 'friend zone,'" she said sternly as Kevin nodded in agreement. I hadn't even agreed to meet the guy and already this was coming up.

Apparently the "friend zone" was something I had become exceptionally good at when it came to guys. At first, I didn't realize this was my M.O., but after Antonia and Laura had both pointed it out (in the form of endlessly making fun of me), I realized they were right—although I would never admit it to their faces.

But these were my high school years—the best times of my life. Why couldn't I just enjoy them with my girlfriends?

"I don't do that," I mumbled not putting up much of a fight.

"Rana, for real, he's an awesome dude. And I'm not just saying that because he's my best friend's little brother," Kevin chimed in.

"Don't bother, Kevin. She's still hung up on Ryyyyyyyyyan," Antonia teased.

"Tonia! I am not."

"Yeah, right. I know you write about him in your diary. You haven't even dated anyone since he moved away- admit it, you still love him!"

Kevin chuckled as he looked at his pager.

"So, what if I haven't dated anyone—I'm enjoying being single instead of getting tangled up in so much drama!" I said, eyeing her and Kevin in the hammock. "And you better not be reading my diary!"

Weeks later, I finally agreed to meet Bronson. At first sight, I was unsure--he was definitely cute, but he wasn't my type. He was blonde, for one, and he dressed very 'preppy' in plaid cargo shorts and a tucked-in collared shirt. He would fit in a Ralph Lauren catalogue perfectly.

But on our first date his hazel eyes, flawless skin, and warm smile started to grow on me.

Despite the snooty school he was from, he seemed sweet. And although I would never admit it to her face, maybe Antonia was right...

A few dates in, I knew I really liked Bronson. He was polite, always holding doors open for me and letting me choose what we would do. He was also super smart; he was on track to become valedictorian and was already getting letters from colleges. Plus, we never really argued about anything. Things with Bronson were just, well, easy.

This was my chance for a fresh start with someone new. It was time to let go of the past. Ryan got a new beginning, why didn't I deserve one, too?

"So, did you like the movie?" Bronson asked as we strolled to his car. We were on our fourth date and had just seen *The Blair Witch Project*.

"Um, yeah it was...definitely scary."

"OK, I have a confession to make. I wanted to see it because I thought you might get scared and grab onto me and all that stuff. Is that corny and weird?" he asked, blushing.

Sort of, I thought. But I was really starting to like Bronson, so I lied.

"No, it's not."

He stopped at the passenger door to his car and turned toward me. I knew what was coming, but I didn't stop it. It was time to take our relationship to the next level.

He kissed me softly. Slowly. It felt nice.

I miss Ryan.

What the heck, get OUT of my head! I opened my eyes afraid Bronson could actually hear my thoughts. He pulled away, a smile plastered on his face.

"Kissing you is all I could think about this past week," he whispered.

"Yeah. Me too." I stuttered, trying to sound convincing. But the truth was I was completely distracted. What had just happened?

After Bronson dropped me off, I scooted past my parents with a lightning fast, "Hi guys!" and was relieved to hear the phone was free when I picked it up. I needed to call Laura immediately.

123

She answered on the third ring.

"Laura?"

"Hey Rana—how was the movie?"

"It was good. Scary. Look Laura, I didn't call to talk about the movie."

"Sorry, it's just I've realllllllyyy been wanting to see it, but Derek doesn't want to so we had to go and see *American Pie,* which was surprisingly funny but actually kind of gross. So, I held my tongue and let him choose. Again. Actually, he didn't choose the movie this time his cousin's girlfriend did. She's such a snob. Refused to share her popcorn and practically— "

"Laura!"

"Was I rambling??"

"Kinda."

"Sorry, you were saying...wait, what were you saying? Derek, hold on, it's Rana I'll just be another minute. I'm sorry, continue," she said, returning her attention back to me. Truth be told, I never felt like I had Laura's full attention anymore, now that Derek never left her side. It's not that I didn't like the guy, but sometimes it would be nice to have her all to myself like it used to be in middle school. Funny thing is, she swore she would never become *that* girl; the one who forgot all about her girlfriends when they were in a relationship. I didn't have the heart to tell her that she was on a slippery slope.

"Well after the movie something happened between Bronson and me."

"Please tell me you kissed him! I want to know that you are actually kissing boys these days!"

Laura's dramatics gave me the giggles.

"Yes, OK? We kissed."

"Thank God! Derek, Rana kissed someone!"

"Shhhh, Laura! Can you not announce it to the whole world, please?" I whispered into the phone. I was huddled on the pink beanbag chair in my room, but I was still afraid my parents might hear something.

Paying no attention, she continued, "So, how was it? Was it slow or fast? Did he do that obnoxious thing boys sometimes do and try and suck your face off or— "

"No! It was...nice."

"Nice?"

"Yeah, it was soft and gentle. He's definitely a good kisser..."

"Then what's the problem?"

"What?"

"There's a 'but' coming. I can feel it. You sound off. You're going to find something wrong with Bronson just like you do every other guy. You don't like him, do you?"

"Laura, relax. It's not like that. I told you, I really like Bronson," I trailed off.

"Well then what is it?" Laura asked.

"Promise you won't freak out on me, Lor."

"Okayyyyyy," she said softly.

"As I was, ya know, kissing him, something, err some*one* popped into my head."

Laura let out a big sigh.

"Ryan Cavanaugh."

"Wait, how'd you know?"

"Derek never mind, this is going to take a while," she said exasperated.

"Laura, help me! My brains messed up! I am not right in the head. Ryan is still somehow dictating my life that I haven't seen in like eight months and suddenly, he's back in my head. I guess I'm still not over him? If you think about it, I haven't been his girlfriend in like three years or something like that. This is what a crazy person looks like!"

Silence.

"Laura?"

"I'm here."

"You don't have anything to say about all this?"

"Look Rain, I'm just glad you're finally admitting it. It's been like forever since you and Ryan were a thing, but you always refused to acknowledge the fact that you never got over him. It's been beyond frustrating that you couldn't see it, but everyone around you could!"

"Gee, sorry it's been so tough on you," I snorted.

"I'm not saying that! I think that the first step in getting over him is admitting it. So, you finally came clean about still having the hots for Ryan, now maybe you can move on. Ya know?"

I hesitated. I knew she was right, but still, it was hard to acknowledge.

"Yeah, maybe..." I replied.

Laura sighed.

"Now, what are you going to do about Bronson?"

"Ugh, I don't know. I feel so terrible. He really likes me and then this happens!"

"Totally. But I still think you should give it a try. He sounds like such a good guy. And Ryan's out of the picture, Rana. Bronson's here, and he's clearly really into you."

I paused. She was right about all of it.

"I want to see you happy, Rana. You deserve it," she said empathetically. "Plus, now we can double date!"

I smiled.

She laughed. "It's settled then, right? You're going to suck face with Bronson and make him your first actual boyfriend?"

"I've had a boyfriend."

"Middle school does not count, Rana, for the love of God, please let it go!!"

"OK, geez, it doesn't count..." I murmured.

"Thank you."

"I gotta go." I replied. "Thanks for talking some sense into me.

"That's what I'm here for," Laura said.

♥ GROWN UP US – CHRISTMAS DAY, 2008 ♥
#SPEECHLESS

Did she really mean it? I re-read the text:

All I know is that I want to be with you. IDK what else to sat

That was one hell of a text to wake up to. The typo made me smile, but I was truly speechless. How should I respond?

I stared at my phone for a few seconds then tossed it aside. The crisp, cool morning air made it easy to stay bundled up under the covers. I must have fallen asleep before she sent the text. I'm sure she was wondering why I hadn't responded yet.

This Rana situation felt like déjà vu in many ways. She had a record of changing her mind and leaving people out to dry, especially me. Maybe this was all some kind of weird nostalgia for her?

It's not that the thought of having a relationship with Rana wasn't appealing. It was. In fact, I was sure I'd waited more than a decade for her to say this very thing. And now she was waiting on *me*. I'd be lying if I said I didn't find satisfaction in that.

But a long-distance relationship? I needed to think that through. With her in L.A. and me in Cleveland, it's not like we could get in the car and take a road trip to see one another for the weekend. We'd be a plane ride away. And let's be honest, we'd barely see each other—the cost, our jobs—it's not like I could just skip out on a week of school or she could leave in the middle of film production. What if we got into a fight? Without seeing each other, an argument could persist for weeks. I also couldn't get over a past experience that left a sour taste in my mouth. Let's just say I know all about how bad long distance could get.

Secondly, there was April. Crap!

April had been in my life for two months. But that didn't really hold a candle to sixteen years. I shook my head at that thought: I couldn't stop thinking about a girl I fell for in the fourth grade.

What the hell was wrong with me? April was a beautiful girl who was head over heels for me.

On paper, she was perfect. Great body, awesome PR job, and she really liked me. For goodness sake, my biggest complaint was that she talked me into going to the symphony. As I suspected, it was incredibly boring, but it wasn't all bad—we kissed for the first time later that night. Sure, it was a little awkward, but we got better at it. And now we're completely comfortable with one another.

Perhaps a little *too* comfortable.

I recently discovered a small cosmetic bag underneath my sink with a travel toothbrush, toothpaste, makeup remover wipes and tampons. It was a startling discovery, especially when I only wanted to find tub cleaner. I thought maybe I should confront April about it since it had seemed a little fast; she hadn't even stayed the night yet. But she'd already left for D.C. when I found it, so I was planning to address it when she got back. If she'd even be willing to see me again after she finds out what happened the other night with Rana. She'll hate me. And I wouldn't blame her.

But at this point, what did it matter? I'd probably mess everything up with her and with Rana—I felt like I already had.

Maybe I should just stick with April and come clean. Hopefully she'll forgive me, and we can move on.

My phone vibrated.

"Speak of the devil."

DECEMBER 16, 2000, SENIOR YEAR
#HomeForTheHolidays

"What are you doing next weekend?" I asked Laura. "I was thinking the four of us could go and see those Christmas lights by the lake. They're lighting up that tree in the square, too," I said as we strolled through the empty halls waiting for cheerleading practice to start.

We had been doing the double date thing almost once a week. Much to our relief, Bronson and Derek got along well and sometimes would even get together without Laura and me. I loved that Bronson and my friends got along. Laura was right, he was the final push I needed to forget about what's-his-face once and for all.

Bronson and I had gotten so hot and heavy that we recently started talking about going all the way. A threshold Laura and Derek had crossed a little while back. We had certainly done 'stuff,' but nothing I would spell out in graphic detail the way Laura (and Antonia) wanted. He wasn't pressuring me or anything, but almost everyone I knew had taken the plunge. I felt a little like being on the outside off an exclusive club. As much as I didn't want to admit it, I was starting to feel left out.

Seemingly ignoring my question, Laura said, "Oh hey, did you hear that Mr. Posser is dating that new geometry teacher? They're like eighty. So gross."

We both laughed.

131

"So anyways, are you guys busy next weekend?" I asked again.

"Who, me and Derek? Um, he definitely does have something to do, and I, I don't know about me yet," she said digging in her purse. Something felt off. Was she avoiding eye contact with me?

We made our way into the gymnasium and saw our squad was beginning to stretch.

"Hi Girls!" Laura shouted.

"Hey everyone," I said. We exchanged pleasantries and got down on the mats to join them.

The gymnasium was stuffy as usual. Our mascot, the bald eagle, covered the walls and bleachers, right alongside our school colors: green and gold, which I despised. They were more like a hunter green and a bright yellow shade—who on earth wears that combo well?

It felt like Laura was still sidestepping my question about next weekend. I sat in a straddle reaching over to one side, then the other, looking her way. She had moved over to chat with another group of girls.

"Hey Laura!" I hollered. She turned to look at me and I motioned for her to come closer.

She made her way over.

"Yeah?"

"Soooo what did you mean when you said you didn't know if you were free next weekend?" I asked.

"I didn't say that."

"You kinda did."

"Hello ladies!" Meryl plopped down right next to us. She was a senior and our squad's captain. She was nice enough, but very bubbly. Like all the time. "What's the 411?"

"Not much, just getting ready for Christmas break. I cannot wait to have two weeks off," Laura moaned.

"Well remember, we still have practice," she corrected. Her long, red ponytail bouncing as she spoke.

"Oh right, what I meant was that I'm anxious to have two weeks off from *school*, not practice," Laura rolled her eyes at me as I tried not to laugh.

"Meryl! Come and check this CD, our warm-up songs are skipping again," another cheerleader complained.

"Be right there! Gotta go, a captain's duty never ends!" she said running off.

"You can't stand her," I chuckled.

"Oh, like you can!" Laura retaliated.

We shared a laugh.

"Lor, is there something you want to tell me?"

She paused for a moment, then looked me square in the eye. It made me kind of nervous.

"Well?"

"OK, I'm going to give it to you straight," she started.

I nodded.

"Because you can handle it. You and Bronson are getting very serious, I think we're over the hump."

"What hump?"

"The Ryan Cavanaugh one," she replied.

I hadn't heard his name in a while, but the sound of it still made me wince. She definitely had my full attention now. My brain was reeling: was he sick, dying, still in love with me?

"Tell me," I demanded.

"Derek and I are hanging out with Ryan next weekend. He's coming back for Christmas break," she blurted out. "I wasn't sure if

I should go or not until I talked to you but I kinda told Derek I would. But I can totally cancel if you want me to! Either way, we can't hang out as a foursome next weekend," she said quietly.

I always had a feeling Derek had stayed in touch with Ryan. They had been good friends before Ryan left—they played football together and Ryan was partially responsible for hooking Derek up with Laura last year.

I looked down at my legs and pulled back on my toes anything to avoid looking at Laura as I tried to process how this made me feel. I never really thought about Ryan coming back to visit his extended family. Naïvely, I figured I'd never see him again. But that would have been too easy. Now that he was going to be here, I wasn't going to let that complicate things.

I looked at Laura.

"I'm going to see the lights by the lake with my boyfriend. Who I like. A lot. You go with Derek and... whoever else, and have a good time. Tell Ryan I said 'hi.'"

Laura looked puzzled.

"You're sure?"

"I'm positive. I can handle this, you're right. Ryan is going to come back for visits. This is where he's from. I was going to have to deal with this at some point. Besides, I have Bronson now. We're in a really good place. I mean, we're even thinking about going all the way."

"I know Rana! I can't wait to hear about it when you do."

"That's like, really serious. That's what boyfriends and girlfriends do," I said reassuring myself.

"Yep."

I reached up and out into a pike position planting my face into my knees and grabbing my feet. My brain started spinning. Ryan's going to be here, like HERE, a mile or two away. What if I just stopped by wherever Laura and Derek were meeting him to say hi? Quick, hey how's it going, then peace out. I'm with Bronson now, it doesn't matter if I see Ryan, we still don't have any feelings for each other...right?

I sat up.

"Rana, are you really OK with this? Because you're doing that thing where you're telling yourself it's OK to like someone else."

Dammit, she saw right through me.

I crossed my feet and sat up.

"I have to see him."

"You what?"

"Laura, I have to see Ryan. It's the only way I'll know if I don't have any feelings for him anymore. And if I don't, maybe I'll know it's time to forge ahead with the whole Bronson-doin-it'-thing," I said, gesturing way too much with my hands. Something I did when emotions were running high.

"You're officially nuts," Laura said, shrugging me off and putting her hair up with her scrunchie.

"No, actually this is making a lot of sense. It's so clear to me," I said with sudden realization.

"You're going to have sex with Bronson based off how you feel when you see your ex-boyfriend?"

"Middle school doesn't count, remember? He's not my ex, he's just some guy," I replied using her own words against her.

"OK...whatever you say, he's just 'some guy'...You sound like a crazy person, you do know that, right? Besides, you don't even know if he wants to see you. You told me your last interaction wasn't exactly friendly," she reminded me.

I remembered the day in the hallway when we said goodbye. And let's face it, he was coming back to town and hadn't even told me about it. Laura was right, he probably didn't even want to see me. But now I was convinced I had to see him, even if he hadn't reached out to me.

"I'll surprise him!" I exclaimed. "Where are you guys hanging out, what's the plan?"

"Oh no, you're not dragging me and Derek into this, Rana. I can't do that."

"Spare me, Laura. I'm not dragging Derek into this, he doesn't even need to know about the plan. I'm only dragging—I mean—*asking* you, my best friend in the whole wide world, to help me surprise a guy I used to know, to see if I actually have any feelings toward him so I can know whether I should consider sleeping with my current boyfriend."

She looked at me with eyebrows raised. I could tell what she was thinking.

"OK, I heard what it actually sounded like," I said.

"So now you see how whacko this is, right?"

"I do," I nodded.

"Oh, thank God."

"Now are you guys driving separately or picking him up?"

Her face disappeared into her hands.

As that next weekend approached, I patted myself on the back for coming up with a foolproof plan. Laura was still a little hesitant, but had reluctantly agreed to help.

Since Laura, Derek, and Ryan were going to be at the mall before catching a movie, I'd casually bump into them around 6:55 in front of Dillard's. This way, Derek didn't have to know about the plan, and Laura and I could act like it was a huge coincidence.

I often wondered if Laura told Derek the details of our private conversations. In particular, I was curious to know if Derek knew about my messed-up feelings toward Ryan. And if he did, would he tell Ryan the truth? I was dying to ask a million questions like—did Ryan ever ask about me? —but I know that would be like opening a Pandora's box. I told Bronson I needed to get a little shopping done before we met up for the Christmas lights. Since I left it vague he probably figured I was getting him a Christmas present, which gave me a twinge of guilt.

I put on my blue, V-neck sweater and my best jeans, trying to convince myself that I wanted to look good for Bronson who I'd be seeing later that night. But a part of me knew it was also so Ryan would regret treating me like he did the last time we saw each other.

It had started to snow as I got in the car to drive to Dillard's. Driving down the icy streets, I began to question how well this would work. Would Ryan see through me? What if he acted like he did before—could I handle it?

It was exactly 6:40 when I pulled into the mall parking lot. As I shut off the car I reapplied my lip liner and lipstick.

"It's perfectly fine that I want to look good," I said out loud to the mirror. I would be wearing this even if I weren't about to see Ryan.

I was proud of myself for remembering to wear a watch. I didn't like them. The tightness around my wrist, the always having someone ask you for the time. It was a responsibility I'd rather not have. But tonight, I couldn't risk being a minute late.

By 6:47 I was walking along the perfume counter of the department store killing time. Oh man, Laura better be on time. Being punctual wasn't one of her best traits, but I was hoping she'd make an exception tonight.

I pretended to browse through some folded jeans as I moved closer to the front of the store. My watch read 6:54. I took a deep breath as I prepared to make my move.

I walked casually to our meeting place—right near the mall entrance. Through the throngs of Christmas shoppers, I spotted Laura and Derek coming towards me. I thought I also saw the top of Ryan's head behind them and I immediately felt tingles all over.

Keeping it cool, I walked their way.

"Oh hey, guys!" I said as I approached them, trying to sound surprised. Ryan was with them, but he wasn't alone. My stomach dropped—was that Natasha?

"Rana, hi!" Laura replied. I gave her a hug while we both delivered our best funny-seeing-you-here performance.

"Hi Rana. I thought you were busy tonight?" Derek asked confused. Laura nudged him.

"Ryan. Hi. It's so good to see you," I said. "Been a long time," I said fingering my hair behind my ear.

"Rana, wow, it's good to see you, too. You look nice," Ryan said.

He looked nice. His hair was a little longer, and he slicked it straight back in a way that made him look older. I think he had gotten hotter in the time since I'd last seen him—something I didn't think was possible. His puffy coat was blocking most of his top half, but I could see enough. Milwaukee was certainly treating him well.

"Oh, thanks," I replied sheepishly, looking down at myself like I had just thrown my outfit together.

"What's up, Rana," Natasha jumped in, clearly trying to appease Ryan. She was still such a huge phony. I hoped Ryan could finally see it.

She had spent the last couple of years doing her best to ignore me. I wouldn't have cared, but I knew that she constantly trash-talked me behind my back. She tried to spread rumors about me on two separate occasions that I knew of, one that involved me suffering from a horrible case of diarrhea after I couldn't cheer at a football game in the fall. She was my sworn enemy if I ever had one.

Laura shot me a helpless look as I tried to figure out Natasha's role in all of this.

Natasha's hair was neatly done in a French braid and her perfume was nauseatingly strong. Her red silk blouse was unbuttoned to show off the top of her black lacy bra. She even carried her coat in her arms so her boobs would be front and center.

Natasha knew what she was doing, and so did I. She was determined to be right there when Ryan came back to town so she could hook up with him. She probably told him she had been waiting for him, but we all knew that her main hobby was getting freaky behind the bleachers after school.

"Oh hey, Natasha." I said, then quickly turned back to Ryan. I wasn't going to let Natasha derail my plans for tonight.

"So now that I think of it, I remember Laura saying you might be coming into town,"

"Right. Remember I told you that Ryan might be coming into town?" Laura sputtered out. Derek rolled his eyes.

Boy she really stunk at this game. I smiled. "So how long are you in town for?" How many times could we say the word "town" in 3 minutes.

"Just for the week. For Christmas," Ryan replied.

"Ah yes, for the holidays," I said, silently sizing up Ryan and Natasha. Were they just friends or was there something really going on between the two of them? And how would I feel about it if there was?

We sat in awkward silence for a moment before Laura interrupted it, "So our movie starts soon," she said, looking at Derek.

"We better get going," Derek replied.

"Yeah, you guys don't want to be late," I said pointing to my watch.

"Since when do you wear a watch?" Ryan quipped.

"Since always," I replied.

"I thought you didn't like the responsibility that comes with them," he mocked.

"Ha!" Laura laughed. I glared at her and she quickly shut her mouth.

"I guess I've been wearing one since you moved away, that's probably why you're surprised," I quipped, knowing that would shut him up.

"Look, I gotta go meet up with some friends. Enjoy the movie," Natasha said as she kissed Ryan on the cheek. Ryan looked at me to gauge my reaction. I looked away, but not quickly enough. Caught red-handed.

"Bye, guys," she waved as she walked away.

Were Ryan and Natasha hooking up or did they just run into each other? Did this mean he didn't have a girlfriend back in Milwaukee? I shook these very inappropriate and unnecessary thoughts from my head. Get it together, Rana, stick to the plan. Nothing more, nothing less.

"So, what do you say, Mancini, you comin' with?" Ryan slyly asked.

"Oh, she has— "Laura started.

"Me? Uh, sure. If that's cool?" I looked around at Derek and Laura, pretending like I cared what they thought.

"I don't care who comes just as long as we don't miss it," Derek grumbled.

"Great! I just have to use that payphone to call my parents. They think I'm on a quick run to the mall," I said pointing to a row of payphones.

"I'll come with," Laura said squeezing my arm and leading me off.

"Ouch, Laura, you're hurting me," I whispered as we walked quickly away.

"What do you think you're doing?" Laura asked as we approached the phone.

"I'm going to a movie with you. And I'm calling Bronson to cancel our plans for tonight, duh."

"Why, Rana? Ryan is here visiting for a week and then he's going back to where he came from. Don't throw away what you and Bronson have on...on whatever this is!"

I picked up the phone.

"Laura, calm down. I'm not throwing anything away I'm just going to a movie. Look, I can't tell if I have feelings for Ryan or not. I need more time with him to figure this out. I should have known I would need more than a two-minute conversation," I reasoned, dialing Bronson's number.

"You are officially full of crap and I am completely wiping my hands of this especially when it backfires!"

"Shhhh! Keep your voice down," I pointed to the phone. Laura shook her head in disbelief. This time, I didn't care about Laura's opinion. Now that I had started this, I was going to finish it. It's what was best for everyone in the end.

"Bronson? Hey, I'm still at the mall but I'm just going to go home from here. Yeah, I'm not feeling well, like, at all. I think I'm getting that flu thing that's been going around at school," I coughed.

I ignored Laura's sarcastic snort.

Bronson was clearly sad not to see me, but he understood. We made plans to hang out later in the week when I was "feeling better."

Laura and I rejoined the boys. I smirked at Ryan as he looked up from his conversation with Derek. I wasn't convinced that I still had feelings for him. As I made eye contact with him, it didn't feel like my insides were swimming. I didn't get lost in his gaze like I always had before. Bronson popped into my mind, and the thought of his sandy blonde hair and his bellowing laugh made me smile. In a way, I was doing this for him. For us. Putting our commitment to the test, and, so far, things were looking good.

"You ready? We've only been waiting for you for like, twenty minutes," Ryan teased.

I had missed his snide remarks and the way he wasn't afraid to put me in my place.

"Ha, yes I'm totally ready," I glanced at Laura who had already vanished into Derek land. Looks like I'd be on my own with Ryan.

Shoot, did that make this a double date?

We entered the dark theatre and Derek led us to one of the front rows on the far left. We all knew this was a prime spot for sucking face without being seen. I tried not to picture the last time Ryan and I did that. I had no idea what *Dude, Where's My Car?* was all about. Another one of Derek's movie picks, so I doubted it would be any good.

"Here, you can sit by Laura," Ryan extended his hand as I followed Derek and Laura in the row. Not that it would matter, she would be making out for the next ninety minutes. Ryan and I sat in an awkward silence as a dancing cheeseburger and milkshake did a skit on the screen. To add insult to injury, Laura and Derek were deep into a conversation that made her giggle profusely. What on earth could be so funny, I just couldn't imagine.

"So how do you like Milwaukee?" I said, finally breaking the silence.

"I love it. It was tough adjusting to everything at first, but this school year has been cool. I made the basketball team so I've been busy with practice. Made some friends."

He was so authentic. He didn't try to act uber cool and distant, he was just himself and he didn't care at all about impressing me. *That* impressed me.

"Nice. I'm glad you're making new friends." Girlfriends? I put the thought out of my head as I quickly switched gears. "And how are your little sisters doing?"

"Ah, they're great. Still cute, but they're really growing up."

Thinking of his little sisters made Ryan's face light up. He was such an awesome big brother. I felt myself smiling warmly back at him.

"Awe, I bet. They were always so adorable."

"And how's everything been going here? Anything...different?" he asked inquisitively.

Yep, I have a boyfriend now.

"Nope, same old stuff. Except Derek and Laura are super serious now," I nodded towards them. We shared a laugh—they didn't even notice we were talking about them.

"Yeah? And how are *you* doing?"

143

"Me? I'm fine. Yeah, things are...fine." Why did I always feel so unsteady around him? He was the only guy on the face of the earth who could make me so nervous. Whenever I was around Bronson or any guy at school I was completely in control.

"I noticed you got your braces off. Your teeth look great."

The mention of my braces instinctively made me run my tongue over my teeth. I had forgotten he hadn't seen me without them. Had it really been that long?

"Thanks," I smiled looking at his long eyelashes. They completely covered his eyes and rested gracefully on his face whenever he looked down or closed them.

There was an awkward pause.

Ryan started in.

"Rana, I've wanted to talk to you about the last time we saw each other that day at school. I know— "

"Rana?" said a familiar voice.

Oh no.

Laura disentangled herself from Derek and whipped her head around to see who was talking. She quickly turned back to me and whispered.

"He definitely saw you."

I slowly looked behind me to see Bronson a few rows back with a bag of popcorn in his hand. "Bronson, hey," is all I could bring myself to say.

"Hey? Aren't you supposed to be home sick?"

"You are?" Ryan asked puzzled. As weird as it was, I felt worse for him than I did for Bronson.

"Well um, not exactly..."

Two of Bronson's buddies plopped down right next to him. Crap, more of an audience to witness this complete train wreck.

The lights dimmed to signal the movie was about to begin.

"Rana, why don't you guys go out in the hall and talk?" Laura whispered, pushing me towards the aisle. "I'll come check on you in a second."

I looked at Bronson who had already gotten up and shoved his popcorn in his friend's lap. I quickly excused myself and followed.

Ryan still looked completely confused as I climbed over him to follow Bronson.

"I'm sorry," I whispered as I excused myself.

I found Bronson sitting on a bench near the men's room.

"Who was that guy?" he asked as I approached.

Middle school boyfriends don't count, middle school boyfriends don't count.

"He's an old friend from elementary school. He moved away and is back in town for a quick visit," I said hoping that was the correct answer.

"Is he here visiting you?"

"What? No," I said adamantly.

"Well I don't know what to believe here, Rana, I mean you cancel a date with me because you're 'not feeling well.' And I find you on a double-date with Laura and Derek, who by the way, is supposed to be my friend."

I shrugged. I was at a loss.

"How can you act like this isn't a big deal?" he demanded, standing up to be level with me. "What the hell is going on?"

I had never seen Bronson so upset. He was usually cool, calm and collected. I think that's partly why I was attracted to him. He was the opposite of my loud, emotional family. Nothing seemed to rattle him. This Bronson, I wasn't used to.

145

"It's not what it looks like. And none of this is Derek's fault, it just happened. I ran into Laura and Derek at the mall and they happened to have this old friend with them. It was a total surprise. None of this was planned, Bronson," I could hear myself making excuses, but on the inside I didn't feel like putting up much of a fight. Did I want to save this?

"Then be honest... were you really sick, or did you just make that whole thing up so you could be here with *him*?" he gestured to the theatre door.

It was my moment of truth. Should I really lie to Bronson's face and build the rest of our relationship on deceit, or should I just come clean?

I heard the door open.

"Rana? Is everything OK?" Laura asked.

Bronson answered before I had the chance.

"No, it's not. We're done here," he said turning to me. "Enjoy your *date*."

DECEMBER 17, 2000, SENIOR YEAR
#EasyWayOut

"Dude, like what the heck?" he asked.

"Man, I don't know. That was some major drama last night and I wasn't ready for it. All I wanted to do was see a movie. Then we run into all these people we know and then Rana gets in trouble with her...boyfriend or whatever?" I said in a way that made it sound like I couldn't care less. But I could.

"Yeah," Derek muttered. He still felt bad whenever he thought about it. He hadn't had the chance to call Bronson and explain he had nothing to do with any of it.

We sat in Derek's basement watching basketball. It was just as I remembered it— a cold, leather couch, small TV, and makeshift weight room. It was nice to be back in my hometown hanging out with my friends again. I missed this. Sure, I met some cool people in Milwaukee, but I hadn't known them for that long. And, besides, we didn't share the same history.

"Rana's boyfriend seemed pretty mad. Whatever, it's none of my business," I shrugged it off. I'll never pretend to understand the likes of Rana Mancini. She was as complicated as they come.

"What's up with you and Natasha?" Derek said, changing the subject. "She was so into you, man. Do you guys still talk?"

I chuckled.

147

"Yeah, we do. She calls me sometimes. We're supposed to hang out later tonight," I said. It's not that I wasn't looking forward to it, I was. She hinted that she wanted to make out, and I probably won't turn her down.

"Nice. I bet you'll get a better view of the bra that was peeking out of her shirt last night," Derek lowered his voice so his stepdad sitting in the kitchen upstairs wouldn't hear.

"I know, I was just thinking that," I said.

"Does Rana know?" Derek asked taking a handful of chips from the bag between them. Derek was a lot sloppier when Laura wasn't around. He would never have worn these baggy sweats if she were here.

"Does Rana know what?" I asked taking some chips from the same bag.

"That you and Natasha have a date tonight," he said shoving some chips into his mouth.

"I don't think so. Unless Natasha told her."

"Trust me, Natasha didn't tell her," Derek replied in between mouthfuls of chips.

"Why not, they still don't talk?"

"Ha! No, bro. Natasha isn't really friends with a whole lot of people anymore. Laura says it's because she's skanky. Oh, come on, that was a total foul!" he screamed at the referee on the screen.

It wasn't the first time I heard that about Natasha. But it was always from other girls. I'll never understand why girls had so much trouble getting along. It was so much easier to be a guy and not be so serious about stuff all the time. Girl World could be so stupid.

"Yeah well, I don't know anything about that," I replied. "She told me she was friends with Rana and Laura and that she liked hanging out with them. I don't know. Maybe the girls are jealous of

Natasha, like she says, or maybe she's the one who's clueless. It doesn't really matter. Rana doesn't know anything about my life and that's fine by me. It gets real old, man. That whole thing." I realized I was talking to myself. Derek was too wrapped up in this Bulls game to have heard anything I just said. It was probably better that way. This crap was getting heavy.

Natasha was fun. I know she got around, but I didn't really care. I certainly wasn't holding out for her. We could just hang out whenever I came back into town. She could do her thing here and I could do my own thing in Milwaukee. This was casual. Natasha was just...nothing like Rana. And frankly, that's why I liked her. With Rana, it was all this history and drama. She could never make up her mind or tell me what she wanted. Everything felt high stakes all the time. With Natasha, it was all so relaxed. Maybe she called, maybe she didn't, maybe we'd hang out, maybe even kiss, it was all whatever and neither of us cared. It was *easy*. I needed that. And I didn't care what Rana knew or if she had a boyfriend or not. I preferred hanging out with the girl who *always* wanted me. With the girl I didn't have to constantly chase after. With the girl that was easy (in more ways than one). And I wasn't going to feel bad about it. Not for one second.

The phone rang and Derek answered it. He mouthed that it was Laura, and I took that as my cue to go.

"All right man, I'll see you," I said, giving him dap. I need to get ready for my date anyway.

As I headed up the stairs and out of the house, I caught myself wondering if Rana called my grandmother's house while I was out. She must have felt the need to explain herself after last night...

JUNE 16, 2001, JUST AFTER HIGH SCHOOL GRADUATION
#PartyTime

It was the first official party of the summer, and we were all celebrating our newly found freedom. Laura and I had been looking
forward to this for weeks. Maybe I would get totally crazy and
make-out with someone. Bronson and I officially broke up the day
after the movie incident—in hindsight, I knew it was never going to
work out, and it didn't take me *that* long to get over him, but I
hadn't dated anyone since. By the time Laura and Derek came to get
me, I was wearing the most killer outfit I could come up with: a long
pink skirt with a white, spaghetti-strap tank top, kitten heels and a
beaded necklace.

I heard the horn beep from my bedroom.

"Bye Dad, bye Mom, I'll check ya later!" I shouted running down
the stairs.

"Whoa, wait!" my dad shouted from the kitchen.

I came to a screeching halt. "Ugh, yes?"

"Are you going to that party down the road?" he quizzed as he
followed me to the front door.

I was headed to Rick Stephen's house. I had grown up with Rick
and ran around in the same circle as him most of our lives. Rick
could always make me laugh, and I will admit I thought about dating
him for a very brief moment when he professed his love for me

150

back in the ninth grade. When I say brief, I mean more like a split second.

His parents were currently on a cruise and his house was enormous; basically, the perfect place and time to throw a party.

"Yes. Why?"

"Because I want to know. And tell them to quiet down. I can hear them all the way up here. Just so you know, I'm not stupid, I know they're drinking. Someone's going to call the police," he said, giving me a look of warning. "And walk home, I don't want you in a car with anyone who's been drinking."

"OK, Dad. I'll waltz in and be the party police. And I'll walk home. Don't worry! Now goodbye, I'll see you later!" I laid a kiss on his cheek and scurried out the door.

"What up, guys?!" I said opening the back door of Derek's car and climbing in.

"Hi, you look awesome!" Laura said from the passenger seat.

"Thanks!" I shouted back over the music. I could barely hear either of them over the Nas CD bumping out of the new sound system Derek just installed his car. Laura looked great, as always. She was still one of the prettiest girls at school. Her brown hair was long and sleek and she wore it up in a ponytail that hung well past her shoulders. Her makeup was subtle yet enhancing, and her lip gloss was as shimmery as it gets. I wasn't surprised at what she was wearing; we'd coordinated on the phone several hours ago.

Although the party was only down the block from my house, Laura and I wanted to make an entrance together—which is why we decided Derek would pick me up on the way. We arrived a mere thirty seconds later and were amazed at all the cars parked in the driveway and spilling down my block.

"Whoa, this really is going to be the party of the century," Derek mused, as we parked on the street and got out of the car.

Rick's house was straight out of the Hollywood hills—huge with a terracotta roof, a perfectly manicured lawn, and a backyard patio that could seat about 50 people. Even from the driveway, we could hear everything: girls laughing, rap music blaring, aluminum cans popping and the guys hooting and howling out back.

"Someone's probably bonging a beer," I said as we hiked up the hill to the house.

"That doesn't sound so bad," Derek smirked.

As we entered the foyer, I couldn't help but imagine what the clean-up would look like tomorrow morning: people were every-where, red plastic cups were strewn on all the furniture, and a blue bag of Cool Ranch Doritos was smashed into the beautiful Persian rug. I immediately recognized a lot of my former classmates. Some were older, some were younger, but mostly everyone was from our grade. I waved to some girls I recognized as the Bauer twins (or, as we used to call, them "the boner twins").

"Rana Mancini?!" I heard a voice shout.

"Josh, hey. How's it goin'?" I met Josh Elmhurst in freshmen year science class. He played soccer, was on the wrestling team and was always very sweet. We weren't the best of friends, but I was pleasant enough towards him.

"Rana Mancini. Wow. I feel like I haven't seen you, in like, for-ever!"

Yep, definitely drunk; it had only been a month since gradua-tion.

He continued.

"Ya know I used to have the hugest crush on you? How have you been?!"

Um, did he mean that? Regardless, I felt flattered.

"I'm good. So anyways, where are you headed this fall?"

Josh opened his mouth to respond, but a fellow soccer player put him in a headlock and dragged him away. Judging by their insults, he was apparently in the middle of a beer pong game.

I headed towards the keg and waited in line for my turn at the Bud Ice.

It's about time, I thought as the last person cleared out in front of me.

"Well, well, well. Look who we have here."

I froze. Oh jeez, doesn't moving away mean anything anymore?

He looked the same: he wore a bright white t-shirt with jeans that had just the right amount of bagginess to them. His Jordan high-tops sparkled, and he had a classy gold chain around his neck that fell into his shirt. His hair was slicked back like when I saw him in December. He was definitely a little more grown up. My eyes filled with mischief. I was happy to see him. And this time there was no Bronson to answer to.

"Ryan Cavanaugh," I said grinning.

"Mancini, what on earth have you been up to?" he said giving me a nudge.

"I've just been hangin' out. How about you, how was graduation?"

"It was good. I got here a few days ago. I'm staying with my grandparents for the summer. And hanging out with friends," he said as he took my cup and filled it up.

'Friends,' huh? I guess I could be considered a friend...

"Really?" I said pulling him to the side. He handed off the hose to the kid behind me.

"Yeah. I'm glad to be done with high school, but I'm going to miss it a little."

There was a group of older girls on the couch that were watching our every move. I'm sure they would all be throwing themselves at Ryan if they had the chance. After all, he was a hot commodity. But I didn't care, this was my time. Ryan was talking to me and tonight I was as free as a bird. This 'chance meeting' could mean our stars were finally aligning.

"You look great," I blurted out.

He chuckled. "Ditto."

'Ditto?' I thought.

"Look, I'm goin' out to the garage for a bit, but it was good seeing you, Mancini" he said giving me a solid hug.

Why did he have to go? He smelled so good. I made sure I wasn't the first to pull away.

Was he mad about the last time we saw each other at the movies? I probably owed him an explanation. Maybe after the drinks started flowing I would catch him and explain everything, but for now, I just let him go.

"Yeah, you too," I replied looking deep into his eyes, hoping he was feeling what I was feeling. But then he turned away and I watched him stroll towards the garage. Just as he was about to open the door, Natasha approached him and they... kissed? Slut! He put his arm around her waist and led her out.

Was I in the Twilight Zone? What did I miss? When did this happen?

I slugged my beer and went for another, staring at the garage door in disbelief. I quickly found Laura and pulled her into the bathroom. "What's going on?" she asked.

I filled her in on everything: Ryan, the hug, his sexiness... Natasha!

"Whoa! I promise you. I didn't even know he was going to be here tonight!" Laura shrieked.

"You swear, Lor? Because I'm feeling a little blindsided here."

"I swear. I heard he might be visiting for the summer, but I had no idea when he was coming home or for how long or anything," she said sincerely. I knew she wouldn't lie to me at a time like this.

"I believe you. What's up with this Natasha thing?" I quizzed.

"I mean, I know they stayed in touch but I didn't know they were...sleeping together or whatever."

"Sleeping together?" I asked, my naivety shining through. I hadn't even thought of that. I guess I just figured that they were maybe in a relationship, but sleeping together?

I hadn't yet given up my 'V-card,' as everyone called it. And in the back of my mind, after everything went south with Bronson, I had started to believe that Ryan and I would be each other's firsts. I mean, sure, geography was a problem now, but not a big one—clearly!

"Rana, you know this isn't the end of the world, right? I don't want to see you upset tonight. Now we're going to go out there and have some fun. Screw him. And Natasha, OK?"

I didn't want to think of Ryan screwing anyone, especially Natasha. But Laura was right, yet again. I wasn't in high school anymore (or junior high for that matter), and this was just stupid middle school drama.

"I know," I said. "I overreacted. We're going to have a good time tonight. And I'm going to get another beer, do you want one?" I asked as I opened the bathroom door.

"Uh, no thanks, I'm still on my first one..."

From the corner of my eye I could see Doug Linder—one of Ryan's closest friends—coming straight for me. I smiled at him from across the room. I had always liked Doug, he was 100% goof ball. By the look of it, he was well past his first beer.

He was tall with dark eyes and a perfect complexion. His dark skin and slim frame was attractive—I could see why he always had a slew of girls after him.

"Rana!" Doug shouted, giving me a sloppy hug as he spilled half of his beer on the kitchen floor.

"Doug! How ya feelin' there buddy?" I asked knowingly.

"Oh man! You have no idea! Hey, you wanna come with me to the tree house? I could really use some fresh air," he sighed.

The fresh air sounded nice right about now. And if I was honest, I wouldn't say no to making out with him if the opportunity arose.

"Um, sure."

"Cool, let's go," he said giggling as he staggered outside. "I was in there earlier making out with Ashley Tucker!"

OK, never mind on the make out idea.

"Nice," I said half amused, hoping he wasn't about to puke on me.

Old and dilapidated, the treehouse in Rick's backyard had seen better days. As I climbed the rickety ladder, I started to freak out about the creepy things that might be living in the rotted wood. Plus, the thing looked like it could easily collapse with us in it. But it was built over the back patio and was a great lookout point from which to see the crowd without anyone seeing us. Standing up there, I saw just how many people were at this party—but Ryan and Natasha were nowhere in sight.

Doug and I caught up on life and our college plans. He was going to the University of Cincinnati to study history while I had enrolled in the fashion program at Kent. Finally, I gained the courage to ask him what I had been thinking about for the last half hour.

"Um, how's Ryan doing? I heard he's with Natasha now?" I said pretending to be oblivious.

"Yup. It's been like six months or something,'" Doug said.

They must have started dating around the last time I saw him, I calculated. Would things have panned out differently if I hadn't been with Bronson? Would Ryan and I be the one in a long-distance relationship right now? Making out at this very party?

"Cool. And he's...like, happy with her?" I asked hoping Doug didn't see right through me. Did I want to be with Ryan or did I just not want Natasha's grubby hands all over him? I wasn't sure.

"Honestly, I don't know how he could be. She's jealous and controlling," Doug confessed. "She's always calling him to find out where he is. If I were him, I would have dumped her months ago." I snapped my head around to look at him. I wasn't surprised at all; the Natasha I knew was a bitch. So much of a bitch that I wondered if her interest in Ryan was to spite me. But that wouldn't be giving Ryan any credit. He was obviously a great catch. So why did this feel like a competition?

"But I guess she freaked when he mentioned breaking up." Doug continued. "And then Ryan let it drop. I think he thinks it's easy just to ride it out for a little longer until they go off to college. I keep telling' him: 'man, you gotta get rid of her if you don't like her anymore.' But he's too much of a wuss."

Ryan was SO that guy. He never wanted to hurt anyone's feelings, which I suppose was guy-speak for 'wuss.'

That said, I still didn't get it. Ryan and Natasha as a couple didn't make sense. How in the world did they wind up together?

"I don't mean to sound like...mean or anything, but, Doug, why is he with her in the first place? She doesn't seem like his type," I said. Maybe Doug could shed some light on the whole situation.

Doug smirked.

"It's what everyone has been wondering. But I guess 'opposites attract.' And the guy has nothing to compare it to. Let's face it he's never had a serious relationship with anyone. Well, besides you."

I couldn't help but smile. Good thing it was dark in here. I looked into my plastic cup of foamy beer.

Doug continued. "He wasn't having much luck connecting with any girls in Milwaukee. Not that they weren't trying to connect, because they were—I heard all the stories!"

My smile disappeared.

"OK, and?" I probed.

"Well Natasha was there. She called all the time, wrote a bunch of emails. I think Ryan was just homesick, he just craved something familiar, ya know?"

"I see."

"That's my theory anyway. And now, he thinks he can change her. She can be such a bitch, but I think he wants to like, love all that bitchiness out of her or something crazy. Dude is in deep," Doug laughed, chugging the rest of his beer. He let out a belch and leaned back against the cracked wooden doorway.

"Yeah, totally," I said nonchalantly.

Nothing Doug said shocked me. Ryan always chose to see the good in people. Even her.

But I couldn't help wondering, while he remains faithful and devoted in Milwaukee, is she completely committed to him.

For Natasha, this was about winning. Nabbing the hottest guy who went to our school was some bizarre feat for her. But her jealous outbursts made it sound like she was letting this little power trip go to her head.

We both sat in silence for a few minutes. I scanned the crowd looking for the not-so-happy couple.

When I finally spotted them, they weren't even touching. Ryan was generally very affectionate. But tonight, he was talking to friends with his back to Natasha, and she was acting like his trophy just... hovering. Gross. No wonder he was sick of her. I watched as Ryan started to head inside. Natasha moved to go with him, but he turned to her and motioned for her to let him go by himself. She scowled and took a seat in a lawn chair, looking pissed.

Yes! They were separated at last. Time to make my move.

"Well, thanks for the company Doug-y, I'm goin' to get another beer. Want one?"

"Nah...I'm just gonna... lay down in here for a minute. You go 'head," he said lazily.

I'll have to remember to come check on him at some point, I thought to myself.

I climbed down the ladder and dashed into the house, like a woman on a mission. Where did he go? Not to get a beer or to the kitchen.

Just then, I saw a hand slide up the banister heading upstairs. I darted over, just in time to see Ryan climb the last step and turn right. I tiptoed up the stairs, following him. After turning, I found myself in the master bedroom. What an ideal setting, I thought. Maybe this was fate. The light was on in the bathroom and I felt butterflies in my stomach as I waited for him to come out. I sat on the bed listening as he turned the faucet on, then off. Laura would kill me if she knew what I was up to.

Ryan swung open the door with a beer in his hand.

"Whoa! Rana, you scared me. You need to use the bathroom too?" Ryan asked.

How naïve, I thought.

"Uh, no," I got up and slowly walked over to him, turning my confidence level to full blast.

He looked at me curiously. I had to think of something clever and sexy to say. Shouldn't be too hard.

"Let's just say if your girlfriend wasn't downstairs right now, I'd kiss you," I said hoping he'd find it sexy to see me taking charge. Endearing. It was after all, true.

Ryan's expression quickly changed. He seemed...disgusted?

"I, I gotta go."

"But— "

"Rana, I'm leaving." He turned and hurried out the door.

I slowly lowered myself onto the bed. What had just happened? I knew he wasn't happy with Natasha. Doug had just told me so.

I felt confused, numb, alone.

I'm not sure how long I sat there, stunned, before some loud drunken party goers came crashing into the room, clearly looking for a make-out spot. I quickly picked myself up and darted down the stairs and out the front door. I needed to get out of there.

As I headed home, the sound of my heartbeat got louder and louder until it was pounding in my ears. How did it get to this? It was probably the last shot I ever had with Ryan and I blew it. He wouldn't do anything to hurt Natasha—even if he didn't want to be with her. I felt humiliated.

I was supposed to be the party police, not break up a relationship tonight. Gosh, I couldn't get anything right.

♥ GROWN UP US – DECEMBER 26, 2008 ♥
#WordsOfWisdom

Shopping always made me feel better (I was a fashion major, after all—shopping was part of my job). The Day-After-Christmas crowds didn't bother me nor did the crammed parking lots. I loved hunting for bargains, no matter when.

Working in the wardrobe department of a film meant I was constantly purchasing clothes and accessories at conventional clothing stores, vintage shops and rental houses. When preparing to shoot a movie, the costume designer selects the look and style of the cast's clothing. Some of these clothes are then specially made, but the rest are purchased by costumers or wardrobe stylists, like me, who then presents the purchases to the designer. Unfortunately, we do a lot of the exchanging and returning as well, so it goes without saying, I spent most of my career in stores.

But today was different. I needed some personal retail therapy. I had a few bucks to spend and a few things to return. Bless Gia and Annabelle for thinking of me, but the jeans they gifted me were a little on the small side. OK, a lot.

I was a size 6. This didn't bother me—I was very happy with my body; I considered myself lucky. Living in L.A., I was constantly surrounded by too-thin actresses and models who complained about not fitting into a size double-zero. But I knew I was healthy just as I was. I ate well and enjoyed exercising, especially lifting weights. Oftentimes I'd be one of the only women in the weight room. It took a while to get used to being surrounded by swollen muscle heads with their eyes glued to my butt, but I eventually got over it and even made a few friends.

As my mom and I entered the mall, it occurred to me I would probably run into somebody I knew. This thought made me start to regret just throwing my hair up in a sloppy bun and wearing my comfortable jeans that were sagging in the butt. But, whatever, I wasn't in the mood to care that much.

After browsing through Home Goods so my mom could look at throw pillows, we went into a department store to exchange the size two jeans.

"Wanna grab some lunch? My treat," she said.

"Sure, I'd love to." And I meant that. I missed my mom. She had promised to make it out to L.A. this spring and I was going to hold her to it.

Even though most of my Italian looks came from my dad, I was a lot like my mom in other ways. For one thing, I know I got my will and strength from her. Like me, she had also gone to school for fashion design, but she dropped out before graduating to get married and start her family. Her love of clothes was passed down to me. And from day one, she was my biggest cheerleader when it came to my career. No way I would have been brave enough to move away and follow my dreams without her constant encouragement. I owed her a lot.

But for the past few years, the thought of her being a lonely widow sometimes kept me awake at night, especially since all her children were so far away. Thankfully, her sisters and my grandparents were close by, which gave me some comfort. But still, I wish I could get home more often.

We all knew she'd never date again, let alone remarry. She would always feel a sense of loyalty to my dad. He had been rather old-school when it came to raising a family, and my mom had whole-heartedly embraced it for almost thirty years. But even though she'd never find another husband, she was still ready for some sort of a change. We often joked she could work for me when I had my own fashion line one day. And, who knew, maybe it would come true? She had a great eye and was a fabulous seamstress.

We strolled into the Chili's attached to the mall. It was crammed full of post-holiday shoppers eager to take a break, like us, so we had to wait awhile before finally being seated.

The hostess took us to a small table near the door, and my mom plopped into her seat. Her petite frame was something my sister Antonia had inherited. They were practically twins, with their matching dark, pin-straight hair that grazed their shoulders. My mom made it a point to never leave the house without lipstick and mascara. I felt the same way about bronzer and curled eyelashes.

"I have to make a quick phone call," my mom said. "Zia Maria was thinking about meeting us in a little bit, and I want to tell her where we are." She pressed the phone to her ear, trying to listen above the roar of diners.

As she chatted with my aunt, I looked at my phone to see if I had any messages. I had made a conscious effort not to think about Ryan yesterday. It wasn't that hard because the chaos of Christmas Day was all consuming. Then, after clean-up, my mom and I ended the day pigging out on the couch while watching *National Lam-*

poon's Christmas Vacation, like we did every year. It was a welcome distraction.

I had four text messages waiting. The first was from Gia asking if we were going to get 'dranks' tonight. The second one was from a costume designer out in L.A. who had hired me for a film beginning mid-January. She wanted to chat details after the holiday dust settled. No rest for the wicked, I thought. But the third and fourth messages were from Ryan. I didn't even feel like opening them as I was on a good streak—trying to get him out of my head. Plus, he had the nerve to ignore my last text for almost FORTY-EIGHT HOURS? He was lucky I still had his number in my phone.

Noticing my mom was still in deep conversation, I ordered two waters for us when the waitress approached. As she scurried off, I stared at my phone and the two unopened messages. What the hell, here goes nothing.

Hi.

Boring.

I think we need to talk. In person.

He waited two days and this was it? Why should I see him? To hear Ryan tell me in person we had no chance? No thanks.

"Text from Ryan?" my mom asked, putting her phone back in her purse.

It startled me, I didn't realize I was so deep in thought. My surprised expression must have made her chuckle. "I guess that's a 'yes.'"

I laughed a little too. "Yeah. It's Ryan. He finally got in touch with me after two days of radio silence. Told me we should talk in person."

My mom scanned her menu.

"And what do you think of that, are you going to?"

"Well, I don't know. I'm just so mad at him for ignoring me. And he doesn't want to be with me so what's the point of seeing him? So he can tell me in person? I don't owe him that," I said opening up my menu.

Over the last couple of days, I had been trying not to think about whether I'd be in the same position if I had made my feelings known sooner. Or if maybe this was karma for dumping him several times in middle school, or rejecting him that one Valentine's Day.

"You don't know that, I think you should hear him out. Maybe he changed his mind. Maybe he realizes what a weenie he's been," she said, making herself smile. She put her menu down.

"Are we all set over here?" our bubbly waitress asked, setting two waters on our table.

Of course, I wasn't ready...I was too distracted.

"I am, are you?" my mom asked me.

"Sure, you go first," I said scrambling, nothing sounded good to me right now.

"I'm going to have the Caesar salad," she said.

"Um, me too. Dressing on the side, please." The waitress nodded, then took our menus and headed to the next table.

"What were we saying? Oh right, you're going to meet up with him, aren't you?" she asked recovering her thought.

"I never said that, Ma. I don't think I'm even going to answer his text. He doesn't get to be M.I.A. for however long he wants and then demand I see him when it's convenient for him. No way," I said, waving my phone around in the air.

"Rana, stop playing these games," she said taking my hand. "It's ridiculous. Now I don't know much about dating, but this has got to be tiring. Just hear him out. I'd hate to see you miss out on what could be the best thing that's ever happened to you by being prideful. Trust me, I am well-versed in pride," she spoke like a true Italian. I knew she was referring to the way she and my dad used to fight. Sometimes they would give each other the silent treatment for days. But they would always find a way to break the ice sooner or later, usually through my dad joking around, like hiding behind a door to scare her or sending a note to her via one of us as the carrier. Man, thinking of those memories made me miss him even more.

I looked at her, "You think a relationship with Ryan Cavanaugh could be best thing that's ever happened to me? But what if we can't work it out?" I asked, with a slight edge of panic in my voice.

"Take a chance, you'll never know unless you do."

Her confidence gave me hope. I knew she was right but I still wasn't sure if I could go through with it. In the moment, I said what I knew she wanted to hear, "Ok, Ma. I'll hear him out."

But secretly, I wasn't so sure.

JULY 22, 2001, SUMMER AFTER GRADUATION
#GROWINGUP

After all the planning, cleaning and preparation, my high school graduation party had finally arrived. My mother insisted on inviting the whole neighborhood and anyone else within a fifty-mile radius. Thankfully, I got to include all my friends and decided that, since he was home for the summer, I might as well invite Ryan, too.

It was a huge step for me considering what happened at Rick's party a few weeks ago. But I didn't want to be rude and since all our mutual friends were invited, it was the right thing to do.

Instead of being super excited to get ready for the party, I was dreading the chores my mom was forcing my dad, my siblings, and me to do: sweep the porch, pull weeds from the flowerbed, dust the entire house from top to bottom.

"But NO ONE is even gonna go upstairs!" I protested.

Of course, there would also be the clean-up, but that was never as bad as the groundwork. My three older siblings tried to get out of everything but attending- until my parents reminded them I was there to do it all for their graduation parties. And they were right, I deserved some payback.

All that said, it was always a good time when I was with my friends and family. The party was going to be a blast.

167

After completing all my assigned tasks, I headed upstairs to get dressed. As I decided on my outfit, my mom called from downstairs, "Rana! Get down here, people are starting to pull in the driveway!"

I looked out my bedroom window to see my great-aunt, Florence (or as we called her, 'Auntie') getting out of her white Impala. She was often the first to arrive at any family function, and we had always assumed it was because she didn't have much else going on and looked forward to these times with her great-nieces and nephews. She had never married or had children, so we were a little like her adopted kids. My Nonno's sister, she was one of those old ladies who said whatever she was thinking, but we always thought that was part of her charm. Today, she was carrying a large bag, likely filled with her famous homemade rolls. I smiled.

Next to arrive would be my Nonno and Nonna Petitti, I thought. My Nonno would be holding a big pan full of sausage and peppers or some other Italian dish that my Nonna had made. He would have to make several trips to the car to get everything she brought (trays of cookies, liters of soda, etc.) so I should get downstairs in a hurry.

"OK! I'll be down in a sec!" I hollered back.

Today, I wanted to look sophisticated and smart. I thought my red, sleeveless turtleneck would pair perfectly with my white miniskirt, which, after some back and forth, I finally decided wouldn't be too short for this occasion. I'm sure my mom would agree, but my dad would raise his eyebrows in disapproval.

Oh well, you can't win them all.

I left my hair down to curl naturally and slipped on my gold necklace with an Italy-shaped charm- one of my graduation gifts from my parents.

I took one final look in the mirror. It didn't really matter if he showed up or not. It was polite to invite him, but I'm sure Natasha wouldn't want him to come and that would likely sway his decision to stay home, I rationalized.

"We're here!" I heard my Nonna shout as I was walking down the steps. Ha, I couldn't have timed it better.

The party was great. The food was delicious. Everyone was enjoying themselves, from my grandparents to my youngest cousins. I was making sure to spend time talking to everyone my mom had invited. My friends were mostly hanging out on the back porch, separate from everyone else. I bounced back and forth seamlessly.

I was proud of the way I had taken my mom's advice on how to be a good hostess: greeting everyone, thanking them for coming, and showing them where the food was and where they could sit to eat. My mom winked at me while I was listening to our neighbors, the Wellington's, tell me about their recent trip to the Grand Canyon. But after about ten minutes, I was ready to move on. When I sensed a pause in the conversation after they mentioned their youngest daughter, Sydney, had food poisoning on their last night, I made a break for it.

I snagged a can of Sprite from one of the many coolers and headed to the back porch for a well-deserved break with my friends.

"Hey guys, what's up?" I said opening the door. I was thankful to be able to unwind for a few minutes.

"There she is!" my cousin, Gaetano replied. Even though he was only twenty, he held a can of Budweiser. Our family was relaxed enough that no one questioned what cooler he chose from. But I'm wise enough to know there's a big difference between seventeen and twenty.

"Well, I had to 'mingle,'" I said mocking my mom.

"So, Rana, Gia and I were just having a chat about Ryyyyyannnnn," Antonia sang. "Is he coming or what?"

Truth is, I was wondering the same thing. It was now three hours into the party and he was nowhere in sight.

I had called to invite him last week, after convincing myself I was finally able to speak to him without feeling completely embarrassed. We never mentioned what had happened at Rick's party. I thought about telling him I had made a huge mistake and that after gaining some clarity, I knew I had messed up. But that would probably only make me sound more like the lunatic he thought I was.

I squirmed in the seat, and fiddled with the top of my Sprite can.

"Uh, I doubt he's coming," I replied taking a sip.

"It's cool. Derek told me he might be busy today," Laura cut in. I could tell she was trying to take the pressure off me and I appreciated it. I was relieved no one pressed for more information. In all honesty, he would probably get death threats from Natasha if he chose to come, so it wasn't really a surprise he wasn't here. She hated me more than anything, and if Ryan actually told her what I did at Rick's party, then I'm sure she wanted to kill us both (even if he was innocent).

The party was winding down and some of my older relatives were starting to head out. I spotted my grandparents getting ready to leave, so I ran over to kiss them and thank them again for everything (and to tell my Nonna that her sausage and peppers were the best, as always).

My friends and cousins, on the other hand, were just starting to let their hair down, and the back porch was getting rowdy. Beers were starting to get passed around, even to the high school kids. I knew I had to keep an eye out but most of them lived in our neighborhood so I knew not many of them drove here.

My dad opened the door to the porch.

"Rana, the phone is for you," he said holding it out. He took the opportunity to scan the crowd with an eagle eye to let us know he was watching. I got up from my lawn chair.

"Thanks," I said taking it from him and motioning for him to go back inside.

I stepped out into our yard, away from the crowd.

"Hello?"

"Hey Rana, it's Ryan,"

My mouth dropped open. Why was he calling me?

"Oh hi, what's up?"

"I wanted to let you know that I'm sorry I couldn't make it today. My grandma was in the hospital so we were busy dealing with that..." he trailed off.

"Oh no, I hope she's OK?"

"Yeah, she is now. She had to get her appendix removed, but she's in recovery. I just needed to be here with her," he explained. Did that mean Natasha was by his side?

"Of course, of course. It was nice that you called. You didn't have to, ya know..." I said softly.

"I know. But I wanted to. It's not my style to be a no-call, no-show."

And it wasn't. It was sweet of him to be so considerate especially while he was dealing with a family emergency.

"Well, thank you. I hope she feels better soon. Annnnd, I hope we can get together before you head back to Milwaukee," I decided to be bold. What do I have to lose?

"I don't think so. I'm heading back in a few days and I need to spend the rest of my time here helping my grandma. I decided to cut the summer short."

I was startled for a second but bounced back.

"Totally. I guess I'll catch you on the flip side then, huh?"

"Always. Good luck, Mancini. I'm sure we'll talk soon. And tell your family I said hello."

"You too."

I hung up the phone feeling good. Like I just got closure or something.

He was right, we would talk soon. Because friends do that: they keep in touch, they exchange pleasantries, they have occasional run-ins and everything would be fine. I'm fine. This was a chapter I could finally close with confidence.

I heard my friends on the porch laughing. I headed back to them with pep in my step.

High school was over. Ryan and I were cool. And all was good with the world.

PART III

NOVEMBER 3, 2001, 18 YEARS-OLD
#TheStruggleIsReal

"I just don't understand why you hate school." my mom said.

"Ma, I just don't like Kent. Maybe it would help if I could...go away to college."

"And what good would that do? If you don't like college here, why would you like it somewhere else?"

"I don't know! I just want to travel and see stuff. Maybe study abroad," I said stomping up the stairs. I was getting so tired of talking about college. Although I was sure I wanted to be a fashion major, so far I was only doing prerequisites, and they were a big ol' snooze fest. I buried my head in my pillow.

Good thing I had spent the last half of my summer filling out endless job applications to everywhere within a ten-mile radius. I had been offered a serving job at Cracker Barrel, which I could do it part-time and still work at Gap Kids part-time, too. I took the serving job in hopes that it would make up for the fact I wasn't enrolling for the spring semester.

My master plan was to work enough to save money for a college out of state. I was particularly intrigued at the thought of going out west, and I found myself considering fashion schools in California, even though I had never spent much time there. My parents weren't necessarily against it, but they felt that taking a semester off would 'lessen my chances of going back.' I wasn't concerned. Still, it had become a constant fight in our house recently.

Ryan annoyingly agreed with my parents. We had remained close. Being good friends, no, make that *really* good friends, was a very cool thing. We mostly talked on the phone, as he was in school at Bowling Green, a two-hour drive away. As far as I knew, he was still with Natasha, I often wondered if she knew Ryan and I stayed in touch. My guess was no, but I wouldn't blame him for that. She would probably freak out anyway.

Ryan and I spoke about pretty much everything *except* romantic relationships. I don't know why. For me, I guess I didn't feel comfortable talking about stuff like that with him, but even more so, I didn't want to hear about his escapades. Not to mention, I didn't have a whole lot to report, and he might have plenty to gab about. It was risky to go down that road, for both of us.

He told me I shouldn't leave Kent to move out of state for school, but I think he was just jealous because his college was in a rinky-dink town in nowhere, Ohio. "Your parents are right, you probably won't go back to school once you quit, you should just stay at Kent," he reasoned. He was always the responsible one. He was studying to become a teacher, and I had no doubt he would be a great one someday.

There was a knock at my door.

"Rana? I'm opening the door," my dad warned. He was so afraid of accidentally seeing me in my underwear that he made sure he always announced his entrance.

"What, Dad?"

"Listen, I know you're upset, but you have to understand why we're pushing you to go to school," he said standing at the door.

"Dad, I told you, I'm going to school, just not *next* semester. I want to take a little time off. It's not the end of the world!"

"Yes, you told us that, calm down." He continued, "It's just that taking a semester off from school isn't a good idea for anyone. Not just you. Besides, working two jobs is a lot. It's not going to be very fun. You have the rest of your life to work, you need to be in college planning for a real career."

I sighed as I clenched my pillow tighter and didn't respond. We'd been around this block a million times before, at this point it was like beating a dead horse.

He finally broke the silence. "All right, well that's all I wanted to say. Dinner will be ready soon."

"K."

As he shut the door behind him, I considered what he said about work. Gap Kids isn't that bad, who didn't like folding tiny sweaters? It's not like I was in the same situation as Antonia's friend Bethany who answers phones at a pest control company. Gross.

Ever since graduation five months ago, I had had this yearning to leave home and travel. I wanted to escape my small town of Canton and go somewhere where no one knew me. My brother, Joey went away to college, and Elisha had a lot of great stories to share from her senior road trip with her girlfriends. Both of their adventures sounded thrilling to me. While, I had no idea what it would be like to travel or move away, I wanted to try it. Plus, if I was going to make it in the fashion industry it wasn't going to be in little ol' Canton, Ohio.

I wanted to go make something of myself. Prove to everyone that I was more than just a pretty-faced cheerleader who liked clothes.

I slammed my bedroom door and flipped my radio on. The chorus to *Oops!... I Did It Again* came blaring on, I quickly turned it off.

My eyes squinted at the computer. They were going haywire from staring at it for so long. The desktop was in Elisha's former bedroom. It looked almost exactly as she left it; waterbed and teddy bear wallpaper and all. Lately, I had been spending most of my time in there looking up schools online, especially if I was trying to avoid homework. I also started searching airline websites for the best deals. I knew if I wanted to enroll in a new school by next fall, I needed to see some of them in person.

Living at home while working was paying off. I was hoarding all my money and picking up shifts whenever I could. I had managed to save almost $2,000 over the last couple of months and it was beginning to burn a hole in my pocket.

Roundtrip flights to California were more reasonable than I had imagined. After September 11th, people were more apprehensive about flying, so there were a lot of good deals. I had found a college I liked in San Francisco and wanted to go visit, and four hundred dollars' roundtrip wasn't bad. I could swing that. I wonder if Elisha would come too?

Elisha and I had started to become close in my last year of high school and spent a lot of time together, since she was one of the only people in my life that wasn't in college. Recently, she told me she might want to move with me. She was 25 and newly single, with nothing keeping her in Canton. I had kept her updated about my research, also trying to come up with new reasons why she might want to move with me. "It's so beautiful this time of year," I would say. Although I knew San Francisco was mostly chilly and rainy.

It would be easier moving all the way to the other side of the country if I knew someone was coming with me, and even better if it was one of my sisters.

My mind started to wander. Should I be thinking even bigger? Where in the world would I go, if I could?

I turned back to the computer and thought, while I'm at it, I'll see how much flights to Europe cost... let's try Amsterdam, I've always wanted to go there...

My fingers typed frantically. I picked two random dates and waited patiently while the page loaded.

"$400?" I muttered.

How can this be? I double-checked the destinations and dates. Yep, I was right.

I scrambled for the phone. I needed to call my sister immediately. She just might be crazy enough to go with me.

FEBRUARY 21, 2002, 18 YEARS-OLD
#EuropeHereICome

"Bye, Dad. Bye, Mom," I said kissing them each on the cheek. "Love you both!" I said hopping into Elisha's new boyfriend's car. The last couple of months had been such a whirlwind preparing for our trip: passports, buying backpacks, clothes, researching hostels in various cities, the Euro rail and more. I picked up all the extra shifts I could in preparation so I didn't have to worry about running out of money.

"Bye!" they both said in unison.

"Have fun!" she hollered as she blew kisses our way.

"Yeah, but don't do anything dumb!" my dad shouted. I could tell he was being serious as I waved again to my parents from the back of Stefan's car.

He and Elisha had met two months ago while working together at Outback Steakhouse. They had started dating around the holidays and now they were practically inseparable. Hence why he just *had* to drive us to the airport.

The timing couldn't be worse for a committed relationship. And that went for me, too. Elisha and I were planning on moving to California after we got back from Europe. A boy would totally screw up those plans. Although nothing was set in stone, we were thinking about a mid-summer move so I could enroll in school for the fall semester. I had even started applying to a few colleges with fashion programs and was waiting to hear back.

But today, I tried not to think that far ahead. Besides, we were about to head off to Europe for the next few weeks—the here and now was looking pretty good! "I'll tell Antonia you said goodbye!" my mom interjected. Antonia had caught the measles a week before and was sleeping through our send-off. She really wanted to come but couldn't take that much time off school. Elisha and I assured her that we would go back again soon. This was our first trip to Europe, but I knew it wasn't going to be my last.

My dad came over to the driver's side window. Stefan rolled it down. "Hey Steve, ya sure you don't need earplugs? Driving with these two for an hour up to Cleveland can be painful." My dad refused to call Stefan by his real name. He said it sounded too snooty. When he mocked it he sounded like the English butler from *The Fresh Prince of Bel-Air*.

But my mom had assured Stefan that if my dad gave someone a nickname that means he liked them. And she was right.

Stefan let out a chuckle, unsure if he should laugh at Elisha's expense.

"Dad! You're crazy, now goodbye!" Elisha said from the passenger's seat.

My dad always made joked around to avoid sharing his true feelings, which in this case would probably be, "I'll miss you, both a lot."

I could hardly sit still as we drove. I was so thrilled to be flying to EUROPE. I had only been on a plane a few times in my life. Once when I was little, my mom took me and my sisters to visit Zia Gina in L.A. and the other time was when Laura's family took me to Disneyworld the summer going into seventh grade. This was complete-ly different, plus I was on my own with Elisha flying thousands of miles away from home.

Once we got to Amsterdam, Elisha and I had decided on going with the flow—we had a basic plan in place, but wanted to keep our options open. We knew there were certain countries we wanted to visit, and we knew the name of the hostel we'd be staying at when we first arrived in Amsterdam—but that was about it. We didn't want to stay in one place for more than a few days before hopping on a train and traveling somewhere else.

We followed the advice of our *Visiting Europe* guidebook and packed things we thought we would need, like comfortable boots and winter jackets. We also made sure we coordinated what we packed so our backpacks weren't overloaded. Like, no sense in bringing two hairdryers when we could share.

We took the same approach with our clothes and shoes too. Like, we did not need two blue sweaters with a cowl neck, or two pencil skirts or even two pairs of low-cut jeans. That said, I knew there were certain things we both needed for our nights out on the town. I mean did we both need to bring our tall black boots with the pointy toe? Yes, we did.

However, despite all this careful planning, our bags still weighed in at an outrageous, sixty pounds each. Some might call it foolish (or as my dad said, "just plain stupid") but I called it exercise. Carrying a heavy pack around was sure to get me in tip-top form. It seemed obvious to me.

"So, Rana, are you excited?" Stefan asked.

"Yeah, definitely."

"Cool. I would be too. I'm a little jealous actually."

"Uh huh." I nodded fishing for my Discman in my purse.

"Yeah. I went to Italy to visit my family a few years ago. I loved it."

"Stefan spent an entire month there just like we'll be doing," Elisha pointed out reaching for his hand.

Oh jeez, here was Rana the third wheel again (my dad was right; earplugs were definitely needed).

Although I didn't mean to, I thought of Ryan. It had been weeks since we last spoke and I hadn't had the chance to say goodbye. Elisha and I would only be communicating via email for the next few weeks, so Ryan and I wouldn't have the chance to talk again for a while. He had also seemed a little distant lately and I was wondering if it was because he had met someone new...I immediately put a stop to this train of thought. I wanted to go on this trip with zero baggage (except for the large one I would willingly carry on my back, of course). This was a time for new beginnings, after all!

As the plane slowly ascended into the big, blue sky I got the feeling that Europe would bring me what I had been searching for. Whatever that was.

FEBRUARY 22, 2002, 18 YEARS-OLD
#LoveSlapped

The double doors slid open to reveal the city of Amsterdam.

The cold air, whipped around our faces, but it was awesome: the cobblestone roads, the train tracks, the colorful buildings, it was all so different from anything I'd ever seen before.

"We're not in Kansas anymore," I smirked.

"Definitely not," Elisha replied taking it all in.

The canals were beautiful, the houseboats were quaint and the 'coffee shops' were everywhere. It was stunning.

As we walked to our hostel I couldn't stop staring. I was interested in everything, what people were wearing, eating, what their typical day was like, what they did for fun. What's considered normal here? What's weird? I couldn't wait to know everything.

Everyone we passed on our route didn't seem like they were in any rush. They just walked around going at their own pace, stopping to window shop or politely smile as they passed us.

I was so used to big American cities, like New York, where people would run you over, ignore you and be annoyed if you had the audacity to ask for directions.

We arrived at our hostel, and Elisha and I walked into the lobby. This was going to be our home for the next couple of days. I was expecting it to be a little rundown and dorm-like but it wasn't. It

184

looked more like a hotel: there were couches, large, colorful paintings on the wall, a computer for guests to use and a little station set up with free coffee and tea. Caffeine sounded pretty good right about now: hello, jetlag.

"Hiya!" a blonde girl with a pixie cut shouted from behind the counter.

"Hello," I said as we approached her.

"Aw you gealz checking een?" she replied in accented English.

I smiled. I was so amused to hear an actual Dutch accent, "Why yes, we are."

"This place looks really nice," Elisha said from behind me.

"Oh, eet eez!" she said overhearing. "I know you well find eet most cozen," she said enthusiastically.

Elisha and I gave each other a look as if to say, *this is so cool!*

"OK. Now, hear aw your room keez."

"Oh, we can get our own room? We expected to be in a dorm like-type-thingy with bunk beds," Elisha replied.

"Yeah, we saw a picture on the internet," I chimed in.

"Oh! Well, eet eez your luckee day. You zee, we aw all booked app. You hav-a to geet aw pwiveet rooms for no additeenal chargeez!" she exclaimed jingling the keys and handing them to me.

"Sweet!" I replied. A private room? Score!

I tried hard to focus as she gave us directions to the top floor, but I kept getting the overwhelming sensation that I wouldn't want to leave here in one short month. I wanted to come up with a scheme that kept me here forever.

"This view is amazing," I said looking out onto the great city of Amsterdam from our small, but cozy, room. Just enough space for a bunk bed and a bathroom but it was all we needed.

"Sure is," Elisha replied. "Stefan's going to flip when I tell him about this," she said.

"Well, I'm starving, how about we change and go look for a place to eat some lunch? Or I guess it's pushing dinner time?" I asked changing the subject. I was anxious to walk around the city without my backpack and see what awaited us.

"Yeah, sounds like a plan."

I sat on the floor with my bag and started the daunting task of finding a new outfit. I had planned very carefully how to blend in with Europeans, noting what I should and should not be wearing. I was looking forward to trying everything out.

We decided it would be wise to ask the front desk staff where the locals ate, so we grabbed our stuff and started to make our way downstairs. But as I was strolling down the lobby stairs, I stopped in my tracks when I noticed...him.

I could hardly believe my eyes. I didn't know what to do, but I knew I had to talk to him. As Elisha started chatting with some of the staff, I stood there flabbergasted.

He walked over to the front desk and the girl staffing it handed him his keys. As he and his friend came toward the stairs, he looked at me and our eyes met. His were blue and eerily familiar. Our eyes were locked for only a few seconds, but it felt like hours.

I was blocking him at the bottom of the stairs, but I couldn't move.

"Par 'din, miss" he said, his gaze never faltering.

"Oh, sure, sorry" I said bashfully.

"Tank ya," he said, stopping briefly to acknowledge me.

He reeked of a zesty cologne I'd never smelled before. It was invigorating. I detected an accent but I couldn't tell what it was. *Yet.*

"Yeah," I managed to get out. Man, this guy had guts: he had absolutely no problem looking me straight in the eye without blinking. It was a confidence I found attractive.

He gave me a gentlemanly nod and he and his friend edged past me up the stairs.

I noticed they had the same sort of backpacks Elisha and I had. They must have been backpacking around Europe just like we were, I thought. I wonder if this is their first stop just like us... My head was spinning with possibilities.

I tried to gauge where he was from by what he had on: dark jeans, slightly form-fitting with an almost bell-bottom effect, much different from the baggy ones' American guys wore. His navy-blue t-shirt fit snuggly around his toned arms. His backpack was an army-green color. Was he in some country's military?

"Hey, what's up?" Elisha asked, coming up to me. I snapped out of my reverie.

"Oh! Nothing. What about you- did you find a place to eat?"

"Yeah, they gave us a few places to try out. I was gonna let you choose."

Elisha pulled out a brochure the front desk had given her and started reading down the list of possible cafes.

I looked back up the steps. I felt better knowing I would be sleeping under the same roof as *him*. Somewhere up there he was thinking of me at this exact same moment. I could feel it.

FEBRUARY 23, 2002, 18 YEARS-OLD
#VARSITYBLUES

"She's in Europe, didn't she tell you?" Rana's mom said.

"Oh yeah, I totally forgot," I replied. And I had, the stress must be getting to my brain.

"She won't be back for a whole month, she just left. Do you want her email address? I know she'll be checking it," her mom said on the other end of the phone.

"Um, I think I have it, but thank you, Mrs. Mancini."

"Good, send her an email. I'm sure she'll be glad to hear from someone from home."

"OK, maybe I'll do that."

"Ryan? I'm so sorry to hear about your parents, is it true?" she asked. I could hear the hesitation in her voice.

Ugh. I'd been trying to forget about it. I was sorry to hear the news traveled all the way back to my hometown. "Yeah, it's true. They're splitting up for good this time," I murmured.

"Oh sweetie..."

"It's OK. Things got pretty bad for a while there. This will be better," I said trying to convince myself more than her.

More than anything, I felt bad for my little sisters, Molly and Michelle. Now that me and Jason were out of the house, they'd suffer the most. My heart ached when I thought about them being shuffled back and forth from Milwaukee to Canton splitting the time between our parents. I'd been drowning most of my thoughts in studying, trying to get into the swing of this new spring semester.

"You're right, it's probably for the best," she said reassuringly.

Divorce. I was more than tired of thinking about that one, complicated, earth-shattering word. Who would have known it could have such an impact on my world? I mean, I had a lot of friends who came from divorced families and until now I was clueless as to what they actually went through. I was looking forward to when things would feel normal again. It was a crappy time to be away at college and not at home to shoulder some of the hurt for my sisters, remind them I'll always be here for them.

I first noticed some serious tension between my parents right before we moved to Milwaukee in 11th grade. It was almost like the move was supposed to be some sort of fresh start. But after landing in Milwaukee my dad worked even longer hours, was away most of the time and the distance between my parents eventually became too much to handle. This was of course what I could gather from eavesdropping on my mom's phone calls to my grandma back home. I heard the words, 'resentment,' 'withdrawn' and 'taking me out of the only place I called home.' I didn't know exactly what the truth of the situation was, but it didn't really matter. When I went back to Milwaukee for a visit, my parents sat us down. They explained everything: how they'd always love them, how it was no one's fault and how they'd remain friends for our sake. They didn't want to be the kind of parents who couldn't even be in the same room with each other. My dad was fighting tears, mom seemed angry, and it all seemed so damn unfair.

I was sure now more than ever about my career in teaching. If I could help at least one kid that had to go through something like this then mission accomplished.

"Thanks," I replied to Rana's mom. "My mom is moving home soon, you should call her."

"I definitely will. Thanks for letting me know that, I'd love to reach out to her."

"She'd like that." I waited a beat and then continued, "Well I'll let you go. I have to get to baseball practice."

"No problem, I'll let Rana know you called the next time I speak with her."

"That's OK. I think I'll send her an email. Bye, Mrs. Mancini," I smiled, it had been nice to chat with her.

I wasn't even sure why I was calling Rana other than I needed a friend, someone who understood me. And the sound of her voice always cheered me up.

I hung up the phone and stared up at the top bunk. Sean, my roommate had just left for his girlfriend's place I was invited to tag along, but wasn't really in the mood for socializing.

Her number was still on my phone's screen:

Mancini
494-8267

I sighed and admitted to myself that I missed her.

FEBRUARY 23, 2002, 18 YEARS-OLD
#HelloLover

"Whoa, aren't you a little overdressed for breakfast?" Elisha asked as I stepped out of our tiny bathroom.

"Nope. I don't think so," I said putting my toiletry bag away and sidestepping the question.

"I'm in my pajama bottoms and flip flops," she complained looking down.

"Not a huge deal. Should we go?"

"Ohhhhhh. I see what's going on here. This is about that guy you saw yesterday. Don't think I didn't notice. You're trying to impress him. Oh, that's just too cute!" Elisha exclaimed forcing me into a headlock.

I squirmed to get out of her grip, "You're going to mess up my hair!"

"Don't worry, your pillow did that already!" she hollered squeezing tighter.

"I hate when you do this!" I threw her off me. "You're being such...a big sister. Now stop it," I said combing my hair with my fingers and trying to catch my breath. I hated when she treated me like a little sister, even if I was.

Elisha and I were seven years apart, but with Antonia being in between us, it almost seemed like more. Back home I couldn't go to

191

bars with her, but here I was of legal drinking age, so we were on an even playing field. I was beyond excited to flash my I.D. and get into the clubs.

"Geez, sorry. I was trying to lighten the mood."

"Yeah, well, I just woke up," I scoffed.

"Then let's go get some coffee and fix that. Plus, your boy might be waiting," Elisha mused.

"Ha! Let's hope so," I smiled.

The bar in the hostel made for a nice, cafeteria-style dining room for breakfast. The pool tables were the main focal point of the room, but there were plenty of chairs around and several tables that held all the Dutch breakfast staples: fruit bread, jam, tea. It smelled wonderful. But first things first: coffee.

Well, well, well. Look who just walked in.

"Um, hello?" Elisha said as she followed my eyes over her shoulder. "Is that him over there?" she said pointing to the entry-way of the dining hall.

"Are you insane?!" I said pulling her finger down. "You can't point!"

"Ohmygosh, would you chill out? He didn't see me. Boy, you've got your panties in a twist over this one," Elisha said pouring a cup of coffee.

"I'm chill, I'm chill," I replied gaining my composure as we sat down at a nearby table.

"Maybe you should go talk to him? I mean, he's right there."

I looked over my shoulder and saw him making his way through the small buffet of food they served for breakfast. I watched as he chose tea instead of coffee- how European. He and his friend took a seat at a table across the room. Breakfast was almost over, so it was steadily getting more crowded with last minute stragglers like us.

"I don't know if I can," I moaned putting my head in my hands.

"Sure ya can. Just go over there and ask him if he needs his bread buttered," she winked.

I peaked at her between my fingers, "You can't be serious."

"I don't know! I'm just brainstorming. Besides, I wouldn't know how to pick up a guy, I'm kinda off the market these days," Elisha smiled.

"Oh please, you guys have been dating for a few months. Get over yourself."

"Get over *yourself* and just go and talk to him!" she said ignoring my insult.

I knew she was right; I had to put all pride aside and go over there. But, I was so nervous!

"Rana go- this may be your only chance."

She scared me enough to take action, "OK, fine. I can do this. It's just talking to a guy," I reasoned.

But I was out of practice these days. Laura was so over my dry spell that she pretty much demanded I jump on the bandwagon and lose my virginity while I was in Europe. Our conversation went something along the lines of: "you're the only eighteen-year-old I know who hasn't done the deed," "Doing it in Europe would defi-nitely make for an amazing story," "Just think how memorable it would be!" and so on. Not that this guy was the one to "do the deed," with, I mean I didn't even know him.

The last date I went on was a couple months ago, with a boy who also worked at Cracker Barrel named Joel. As it turns out, Joel was only interested in making out. He practically attacked my face after taking me to Applebee's. Hardly romantic, but I gave in. It was just nice to be kissed. And I could tell he had lots of practice. But when he called the next day to invite me over to "watch a movie" I declined. I knew what that meant, and I wasn't really interested in doing that with Joel. The one-time make-out was all I really wanted.

But now, something was drawing me to this guy. What was it?

"There ya go. That's the right attitude," Elisha said biting into her toast.

"Because I'm in Amsterdam for the first time, and, if not here, then where?" I said pepping myself up.

"All right, his friend just left the table, now's the perfect time," Elisha nudged my foot.

I got up and began making my way through all the tables and chairs that were scattered around the room. I smiled at the other diners as I passed them, trying to feel as confident as I attempted to look. My mouth was as dry as sandpaper.

I approached his table, "Hi. Good morning."

"Hey dair. Good mornin' to ya," he said in his accent. Scottish or Irish? I still couldn't tell. He was so laid back, like a random girl approaching him at breakfast was a normal occurrence. It only made me more nervous.

"Thanks," I replied shaking my head unsure of what I was going to say next. There was a pause that seemed about a month long. I was about to panic and run back to my table.

"OK, well, I- "

"Care to have a dab a tae wit me?"

Tea? A 'dab?' Could he be any cuter?

"So, do ya drink tae? You should take a chair and have some if ya like," he said calmly taking a sip of his. I must have looked like a deer in the headlights.

I never had hot tea in my life. I didn't even know what to do to it. Do I add creamer? Sugar? Do I hold out my pinky finger when I take a sip?

I replied with what only felt natural, "I love tea." Oh, the lies...I pulled out the chair and took a seat across from him. He poured me a cup of dark brown liquid and pushed the sugar and milk towards me.

"I'm not sure how ya take it," he smiled.

"Thank you," I said. I'm not sure how I take it either... I poured in a little milk (or was this half and half?) to match the color of his, then added a small spoonful of sugar and took a drink. Gross! This is disgusting, how have people been drinking this for the last billion years?! I swallowed what was in my mouth and grinned, "Delicious. So, where are you from...I'm sorry, I don't even know your name."

"I'm Paul. Paul Howard. And what's yours?"

"I'm Rana, nice to meet you," I stuck out my hand to shake his. His grip was firm, his big hand was warm, but not sweaty. I liked it.

"Rana? Dat's vary pretty. So, Rana, I'm from Limerick- didcha ever hear of it?" he said. His accent was so thick and he spoke so fast that I had to wait a beat so my brain could catch up.

"That's in Ireland, right?"

"Yeah! Boy, I'm surprised ya know it, it's so tiny," he said beaming. "And you must be from Amurrica?"

"I am," I nodded.

"Wow! I would love to go dair someday. It seems so beautiful."

I loved the way he over-pronounced his T's. "Yeah, it is. There're some beautiful parts. I guess it depends where you go," I said forcing another sip.

"See, it's probably borin' to you because ya live dair, but for someone like me...well, it'd be so amazin,'" he said with such excitement that I couldn't help breaking into a big grin.

I forced more tea into my mouth. "I think you're right, Paul. And I would love to go to Ireland someday. I've heard it's also very beautiful there."

"It is," he smirked looking at me straight in the eye. "And you are also a beauty. Butcha already knew that," he said turning coy.

I squirmed in my seat, touching my hair to keep my hands occupied. "Well, thank you. You're sweet," I replied. I couldn't quite tell if he was genuine or not. Was he a lady's man? Playa? Just a plain slut? Or was this what Irish men were like?

"I may be charmin' but I'm honest," he said grabbing the small teapot and refilling his cup. While he was at it he poured more into mine. I cringed at the thought of having to drink even more of this sludge, but I know he was being thoughtful. And I took it as a sign that he wanted me to stay longer.

"So, what brings you to Amsterdam?" I asked changing the subject.

"Nuttin'. I just wanted to travel. It was getting very...predictable at home," he said searching for words. "I knew I had to get out and do sometin.' Do ya know what I mean, like?"

It sounded just like one of my many journal entries. I chuckled, "Yes, I know *exactly* what you mean. Exactly."

He smiled and nodded looking so deeply into my eyes that I looked away. It was like we didn't have to speak. There was just... an understanding.

"So, Rana- can I take you to dinner tonight? No, lunch? I couldn't possibly wait for the evenin' to get hare," he said winking at me.

I felt pins and needles spread throughout my whole body, and I tried to fight the huge grin that was about to spread across my face. I calmly answered, "Sure," even though my brain was spinning from excitement and possibility.

I wasn't used to a guy being so straightforward. Back home it was more of a dance of sorts... I might like you, but I can't let on to that too much in the beginning type of thing. Even though I felt I had mastered the rules of the game (with maybe even inventing a few of my own), they seemed so stupid now. Like why couldn't dating be this easy all the time?

I stood up and pushed my chair in; I knew I had to be the first one to leave the table. It was a rule my Zia Maria taught me: always be the first one to end the conversation, it leaves them wanting more.

"I'd better get going. Should I meet you in the lobby around noon?"

He stood up to meet my gaze, "Better make it the bar," he said laughing.

"Your Irish reputation precedes you," I smiled, turning around to walk away. I gave myself a virtual high five, pleased that I could end our conversation on a witty note.

"Rana?"

I snapped my head around to look at him.

"It was good to meetcha," he said giving me a gentlemanly nod.

"It was nice meeting you too, Paul."

I turned away and strutted my stuff past the table Elisha was still sitting and straight out the door. I know he watched me the entire way.

<u>12:15PM:</u>

"You better get down there, Rana. You're so late."

"I am not. I'm like 10 minutes late and besides, it's considered 'fashionably late," I retorted.

"Whatever. He's going to think you stood him up and leave."

"Relax, this is Europe, everyone's always running late. It's the culture," I said applying clear lip gloss to accentuate my natural lip color. This was a lunch date, not a dinner date after all.

Elisha rolled her eyes, "I gotta hop in the shower or else I'm gonna be late too."

While I was talking to Paul, Elisha had met a fun group of international travelers at breakfast. They were from all over the world: Brazil, Iceland, and Egypt, and were going to the Heineken Museum this afternoon and then out on the town. Knowing she had people to hang out with made me feel less guilty about ditching her for some random guy.

"Wish me luck!" I said taking a final look at my reflection. The tight jeans I was wearing emphasized all the right things. My black sweater was a little plain looking, so I added a scarf and some dangly earrings.

"Good luck. And stay out in public, don't let him take you into any dark alleys or basements."

"Got it, mom, anything else?"

"Just go!" she said shoving me out the door. "Do you have your purse? Pay your own way, you're in the Netherlands," she joked.

"What, so I should go Dutch? You're such a dork."

I practically skipped down the stairs until I reached the second floor, gathering my composure as I walked into the bar. I looked around and quickly spotted Paul waving at me. He paid the bartender and strolled over to me with two pints of beer.

198

As he stepped out from behind his barstool I got a full body shot and took the opportunity to examine everything. He had the same jeans on as the other day and black Doc Marten boots with a light blue button down that made his eyes pop. He looked great.

As he got closer, I smelled that same spicy cologne as the day before.

"Ya look gorgeous," he said.

"Thank you."

"I got Heineken, do ya like dat? I figured it was a safe bet. Do ya wanna grab a table?"

"Yeah, sure. Is that one okay?" I said pointing at a table in the corner that looked more secluded. Even at this hour, the bar was getting packed. Welcome to Europe, I thought.

"Perfect. Here, have a chair," he said setting down the drinks and pulling out a chair.

"Thank you," I replied. I couldn't remember the last time a guy pulled a chair out for me. Had a guy *ever* done that for me?

"Thank you."

Now what. This moment would be telling. Would we have anything to talk about? Or would this be one giant awkward encounter?

"So, I havta tell ya somethin,'" said Paul.

"Oh, yeah?" I replied feeling a little worried. I mean, it could be anything. Like, was he engaged to another woman and now, after meeting me, realized he couldn't possibly go ahead with the wedding (okay, maybe I shouldn't have watched *The Wedding Planner* on the plane ride over).

"Yeah. This mornin' wasn't the first time I noticed ya. Do you remember dee utter day in da lobby? I had just got hare and I saw ya standin' by da stairs."

I liked the direction this was taking. "I remember. I saw you too," I said relieved, taking a sip of my beer. Back home I would not be in a bar drinking at lunchtime. Then again, at only eighteen, I wouldn't be in a bar drinking at all. I felt so grown-up.

He continued, "Well, I couldn't stop tinkin' aboutcha after dat. I was hoping I'd run into ya again. Dis mornin' when I saw ya eatin' break-fast, I told Gerrod to leave 'cause I was getting' the nerve to come talk to ya. Ya just beat me to it is all."

I was flattered, but was careful to keep my expression only slightly amused so I didn't seem like a dumb American teenager.

"That is...so sweet of you to say," I said fiddling with my glass.

He touched my hand and looked at me as if to say: Stop. Look. Feel. I reluctantly looked in his eyes, and it took everything I had not to giggle.

"I really wanna get to know ya. Can we do dat, like?" he finally said in that sexy accent of his.

"Yes. Definitely," I replied thinking briefly of Elisha. Was I jumping ship when we were supposed to be on this trip together? But then I figured she would be happy for me—and, besides, she has this new group of friends.

"Cheers to dat!" he exclaimed holding up his glass.

And just like that we sealed the deal.

I took a drink and figured I might have to tell Elisha we were staying in Amsterdam longer than we had planned. After all the griping I did about Stefan, I was turning into quite the hypocrite.

4:00PM:

After a long lunch at a casual restaurant a couple of blocks away, we found ourselves roaming the streets. I had absolutely no clue where we were and I didn't particularly care. I felt safe with Paul.

He was twenty-one years old, had a younger sister, loving parents, was adopted and his birthday was on Christmas Eve. Throughout the whole afternoon, there was never an awkward pause in our conversation. It felt like we had known each other for years.

Like us, he and his friend, Gerrod were backpacking around Europe. Amsterdam was also their first stop. They were taking a slightly different route focusing more on Spain and Portugal. Elisha and I didn't know exactly where we were going, however we knew we were definitely hitting Italy, Germany and France. But now things might change...

"So, have you ever been in love?" I asked. I was dying to know if he'd had a girlfriend recently and how long he'd been single.

"Nah. I tink dat love is just an illusion between two fools...I dunno," he replied. "What do you's tink?"

Geez, that was kind of depressing. Was this guy just a cynic? Or had he been burned?

"Well, I believe in love if that's what you mean," I said.

"Huh," he grunted.

Not the reaction a girl would want on a first date. But who's to say I couldn't change his mind?

Paul insisted that I open up about my life and not just ask him all the questions. It was tough but I liked the way he challenged me. I was never very good about opening up to a guy, but he made me feel comfortable.

I told him all about my family, my passion for the fashion industry, how I came up with the idea to come to Europe and how now I
never wanted to go back.

"Would you do dat? Just never go back, like?" he said with a
twinkle in his eye.

I took a pause and carefully considered how to answer. I mean,
I'd love to study fashion in Paris or Milan and I think it would really
give me an edge over the competition, as well as the inspiration to
really go after my dream of starting my own line.

I responded with a line from one of my favorite movies that I
thought would fit perfectly, "I'm a kinda fly-by-the-seat-of-your-
pants gal," I nodded.

I was hoping he didn't recognize the movie, but I remembered
that A) it was a total chick flick, and B) *Pretty Woman* might not be
as popular in Europe, maybe he'd never heard of it.

"You seem really adventurous. I admire dat aboutcha ya know,"
he said giving my hand a squeeze.

Me, adventurous? That's something nobody had ever called
me—I couldn't wait to tell my friends back home.

Mission accomplished. Thank you, Vivian Ward.

The afternoon pressed on and day turned into evening. I figured
Elisha was long back from the museum by now, and perhaps even
getting irritated about not hearing from me. I owed it to her to at
least check in.

"Should we head back now?" I reluctantly asked. I really didn't
want our walk to end, but Zia Maria's rule was flagging in the back
of my mind. Plus, it was starting to get chilly.

"Sure," he answered.

This day had flown by so fast, it almost wasn't fair. My time with Paul was nothing short of magical. I was left wanting more. SO much more. I could hardly believe that this time last week I was stocking shelves at Gap Kids and picking up shifts at Cracker Barrel.

"So, what aboutchu? Ya never answered from before," Paul asked stopping on a little bridge running over the canal. They seemed to be on every block. He turned towards me and rubbed my cold hands in between his.

"Hmm? I never answered what?"

"If you've ever been in love. I know you believe in it, but has it ever bitten ya before," he smirked.

For the first time since arriving in Amsterdam, I thought about Ryan, how if I'd ever been in love, it had only been with him.

"Yeah. I think so," I said.

"Oh?"

"Yeah. But it was a long time ago. I don't even know if it counts."

He looked at me, interested, "Sometin' tells me it does."

I shrugged his statement off and started towards the hostel, but Paul didn't let me go and pulled me in close. He stared into my eyes as my heart thrashed so loudly I was sure he could hear it. He then laid his plump lips on mine and kissed me. It was confident and passionate. His breathing was hurried and his hands slid up my hips. I took it all in and thought, so *this* is how a European boy kisses...

♥ GROWN UP US – DECEMBER 26, 2008 ♥
#PlayOnPlaya

April:

Hi! I miss you, how was your night?

I didn't know how to respond. I wasn't a heartless jerk to dump this on her in a text message. And I was still considering exactly what to do; I could still mend this relationship with April, we had potential. But was I waiting to see what happened with Rana before determining what to do about April?

Either way, I needed to get things sorted out with Rana. She hadn't yet answered my text message about talking in person, and I was trying not to check my phone every ten minutes to see if she had. I was starting to get worried she's sworn me off for good; I'd texted hours ago. Not that she could be blamed, it took me nearly two days to reply to her.

But I needed to know how she really felt about me, to figure it all out. And not over text, I wanted to sit down face to face. Not only was it the adult thing to do, she owed me that after all we've been through.

I sat on my couch and channel surfed to avoid April's text. Finally, I picked up my phone and hit REPLY:

Hi. We should talk when you get home. Can you stop by?

April:

Definitely

REPLY:

Sure. Everything ok?

Dang, juggling two girls was SO not like me. I was acting like the ultimate douche bag.

MARCH 1, 2002, 18 YEARS-OLD
#WhatsInAFace

I missed Paul like crazy.

We had said a dramatic goodbye with a long kiss and a promise that we would keep in touch. Before I boarded the train, he whispered in my ear, "I have a feeling I'll be seein' ya very soooon." And although I had no idea how that would happen, I believed him. Despite hearing Laura in the back of my head, Paul and I didn't "do the deed," but that wasn't to say it couldn't happen at a later date.

I was trying my best to just let go and enjoy the rest of the trip. After all, if Paul and I were going to reconnect, it would happen in its own time.

But everywhere I turned, there he was. I kept thinking I saw him out of the corner of my eye. Even on the train from Germany to Italy, I ordered a beer called, Paulaner (and, of course, it was delish).

When we arrived in Venice, we weren't disappointed. It was incredible: the old, rustic buildings, the gondolas, the cobblestone streets and all the beautiful bridges. Everything was on water—even the taxis were boats! I recognized the sites from books and TV, but also from the cover of my 'Learn Italian!' cassette tapes my Zio Tony had given me.

I had taken several pictures of Paul in Amsterdam and decided that I would get that roll developed sooner rather than later. I was forgetting what he looked like and I desperately needed a visual.

This always happened when I liked a guy; his face became blurred out in all my memories. I specifically remember it happening with Anthony Lucarelli. Since we went to different schools, we would only see each other on the weekends, mostly at the skating rink. All during the week I'd wrack my brain trying to envision his handsome face. It would appear for a split second but then it would slip away again. When he finally gave me a small school picture, I was able to overcome it. Oddly enough, this never really happened with Ryan, even when he moved to Milwaukee. I wondered what he was doing now—had he tried to get in touch with me while I was gone?

#PSIMissYou

March 12, 2002, 13:45
From: Paul Howard- paul_howard@yahoo.com
To: Rana Mancini- fashiongirlrana@yahoo.com

My Dear Rana
Sorry I couldn't respond sooner. Were in a town called Magalluf.
It's a fun part of the island and I wish you were here to see it.
Gerrod thinks I am a fool because I cant stop talking about you.
When are you coming down lol
Love always
Paul
Ps. I miss you

March 13, 2002, 20:08
From: Rana Mancini- fashiongirlrana@yahoo.com
To: Paul Howard- paul_Howard@yahoo.com

Hi Paul,
Magalluf sounds awesome. Hope you're having a really good time.
I am also talking about you a lot but I think my sister is a little more
patient than Gerrod is :)

We are in Brussels and having a lot of fun. I just LOVE all the different kinds of clothes and fashion I'm seeing! Im saving some money to buy something incredible to take back home with me. Haven't seen it yet but I know it's out there. I'm jotting down ideas in my journal every minute I can and I window shop most mornings while Elisha sleeps.

We leave in about a week, trying not to be too bummed. Or maybe I'll come and see what Magalluf is all about haha Talk soon.

Love,

Rana

March 13, 2002. 23:27

From: Paul Howard- paul_Howard@yahoo.com

To: Rana Mancini- fashiongirlrana@yahoo.com

Can you call me tomorrow? You have my number. I want to ask you something. Hope you get this in time.

Paul

March 14, 2002. 16:13

From: Ryan Cavanaugh- rcavanaugh@bgsu.edu

To: Rana Mancini- fashiongirlrana@yahoo.com

Hey Rana,

How are you? I called you a couple of weeks ago but I forgot ur in Europe. Wow I'm so proud of you for going for it. I hope you're having an awesome time. Sorry its been awhile since I called. Things have been really busy. Baseball is taking over my life lately. The conditioning is brutal. I'm heading to Canton next week and wanted to take you to dinner, but I guess you won't be there haha. Just wanted to talk to you. Hope you're having fun. Stay safe and don't do anything I wouldn't do! Write me back.

Love,

Ryan

P.S. I miss you

MARCH 14, 2002, 18 YEARS-OLD
#TheBestLaidPlans

In Paris I was like a kid in a candy store. The clothes. Oh, the clothes. There was a plethora of pencil skirts, pointy shoes, leather wrap belts, wide-legged jeans and elegant headscarves. I was definitely not hip enough for Paris, and I was dying to buy something to better fit in. By this point, I was starting to see fashion in a whole new light and I couldn't wait to start adapting my wardrobe when I got home.

I begged Elisha to come to a fancy boutique with me that had been recommended by a fellow roomie at our hostel. She finally said yes when I mentioned that the café across the street boasted the most amazing French roast. Coffee was always a selling point.

I was secretly hoping that whatever I picked out Paul would see somehow.

"Talk about suspense! I wish he would have just told you what he wanted in the email," Elisha said, holding up a lacy bra in front of herself in the mirror. "When are you going to call him?"

"I think when I get back to the hostel later this afternoon." I replied.

"You would like to try on?" an employee said with broken English.

"Yes, please," Elisha said, going behind the dressing room's paisley curtain.

Until now I had been rummaging through some sweaters in the sale section, but decided to wander over to the lingerie just for kicks. It never occurred to me until I saw Elisha holding that gorgeous bra that I had nothing but raggedy bras and panties in my backpack. There was still a chance (however small) that Paul might actually see my underwear. At least I hoped there was still a chance.

"I'd like to try this on, please," I said getting the young salesgirl's attention.

"Whatcha find?" Elisha called from the dressing room next to mine.

"Oh, nothing," I muttered quickly changing out of my clothes. I stared at myself in the mirror, and I liked what I saw: red, lacy, *skimpy*. This was definitely a look Paul would like.

"So, I got another email today," I confessed as I continued to evaluate my new lingerie.

"From who?"

"Uh, Ryan."

"Cavanaugh? What did he want?"

"Nothing, I guess he was just hoping to catch up. I think he kind of asked me out though."

"Seriously? What now?" she said slipping her curtain open.

"I don't know, it was very casual. Too casual, I almost missed it: I want to take you to dinner, hope you're having fun in Europe, yadda yadda."

"Interesting. And how did he end it?" Elisha asked.

"Well he said 'don't do anything I wouldn't do.' What do you think he meant by that?" I asked.

Elisha slid my curtain open, thankfully I had just changed back into my clothes.

"It means he doesn't want you doin' it with anybody else, is what that means."

Startled, I edged past her holding my sexy new finds. "Don't be ridiculous."

"I'm not. That's what he meant. Trust me. He's trying to keep tabs on you from afar," she nodded her head with certainty.

Was she right, did he really have the nerve to insinuate that I shouldn't sleep with anyone? If I met someone and wanted to go all the way, then I could do what I damn well pleased, I wasn't even on American soil! Ryan and I weren't in a relationship, we weren't even casually dating—we were just friends who talked on the phone every so often.

"That's not all, he said something else, too," I confessed.

"Oh?"

"Yeah. He, um, told me he missed me."

"Are you friggin' kidding me?" Elisha exclaimed. "That boy has got some guts, I'll tell ya that much!"

"I know! We were finally in a good place being just friends and he goes and says that? While I'm in Europe, no less. Does this mean he wants to get back together or was this just an I-miss-you-as-a-friend sort of thing?" I asked impatiently.

"Well now let's examine this carefully. I want you to ask yourself if it really matters."

"Huh?"

"Rana, if he wanted to get back together with you, would you drop everything and do that?"

My mind went blank as other shoppers swarmed around us.

Yes. "I'm not saying that..." I trailed off. "I really like Paul. Like *really* like him," I replied assertively.

Man, I wish I could talk to Laura right now. She would absolutely flip her lid if she knew anything about my current situation. I had been emailing her, Antonia and Annabelle and Gia on a group email, but hadn't yet mentioned Paul. Not only did I not want to jinx what he and I had, I also wasn't ready to be interrogated about it or asked why we hadn't slept together yet.

"Well are you going to email Ryan back?" Elisha asked examining the lingerie I had in my hands.

"Nope." I held up the bra and panties to the saleswoman, "I'd like to pay for this."

I had put Ryan out of my mind for almost the entire trip, and now he's telling me he misses me? I'm not doing this. I'm moving forward with my life. And with Paul.

We headed back to the hostel and got ready for dinner. The phone there wasn't working, so I called Paul from the payphone at the restaurant where we were eating. He picked up on the first ring.

"Hi, Paul?"

"Rana! Lass, I bin waitin' for ya to call all day. Was afraid you didn't get my email or sometin,'" he said.

I gave a sigh of relief, "I got it. How are you?" I replied.

"Very well now that I'm talkin' to ya."

"Thanks, that's so nice of you to say."

"It's true," he replied. "Soooo, have ya givin' anymore tought to comin' down to Mallorca, like?"

Wait, he was serious about that?!

"Uh, no, not really. I mean, a little...Why?"

214

"Just wonderin' like," he muttered. "I guess I don't wantcha to go back home. I want ya here...wit me."

It was one of the sweetest things anyone had ever said to me. There was a sense of confidence in his words—like he knew I was his, even after spending only a few days with me. I could have met someone else for all he knew, but he didn't care. He knew the connection we had was intense and so did I.

"With you?" I responded in disbelief.

"Yeah, like. Do ya have any plans ferr your life?"

I spotted Elisha across the restaurant. She was having a casual conversation with a few guys. They erupted into laughter. She caught my gaze and gave me a thumbs-up as if to say, "everything all good?"

I thought about our plans to move out to California. How exciting it all seemed, but how we hadn't talked about it much lately. And then I thought about Stefan and how he would likely stand in the way of all of it. What if she told me she couldn't move because of him? Going back to work at Gap Kids and continuing with daily life wasn't the right move for me. Besides, wasn't Paul something I'd been hoping for?

I also thought of my career. And college. I needed to finish school or my parents would kill me. I'm sure they would not be happy if I stayed.

I gave Elisha the thumbs-up back. "Uh, no. Not really any plans per se..."

"Ah, dat's great! Come down here, Rana. I'll wait for ya! I tink I got a job and you could get one too. We could live on da beach and have a grand time! Whaddya say, lass?"

#OnMyOwn

It was one heck of a trip. Five trains, one subway and a ferry to be exact. Going from Paris to Mallorca wasn't exactly easy. Throw in not being able to speak the language and it was downright terrifying. It was probably the bravest thing I had ever done. And for what better reason than to take a chance on love?

Elisha was supportive but skeptical, pointing out that we didn't know Paul that well, that college would be put on hold for even longer and that I couldn't get a decent job without a visa. But overall, I think she was a little relieved that I wouldn't be holding her to moving with me to California anytime soon, especially since this trip had proven to her that she didn't like being without Stefan.

When we called my parents to tell them my plan, my dad refused to talk to me saying that he would rather 'address the situation' when I was home. I tried not to think about what that would be like—whenever it happened. My mom was a little more understanding, saying that she trusted me and that she could live without me for a few more months if Paul was a good guy.

The ferry from Barcelona to Mallorca was more like a mini cruise ship with a restaurant, gift shops and plenty of seats. I chose one by the dock and pictured my reunion with Paul like I had a million times in the last month: our eyes would lock, he would sweep me into his arms and lay a kiss on me that was so magical the earth would tilt on its axis, just like the photo of the soldier who returned home from WWII and kissed his lady in the middle of the celebrating Manhattan crowds. Still, I had to admit that a part of me was a little uneasy. What if Elisha is right and Paul was a total psycho? What if he didn't show up and this was all a joke? What if he changed his mind and ended up not liking me after all? This was so risky. And grownup. But I had made a decision, and now I had to make the best of it.

Ah, the pre-selfie days

When I arrived, we would be staying in a hotel together and one thing could lead to another. I had never done that with a guy before, and I was a little nervous about it. I pondered this while I looked out at the sea. A goofy grin appeared on my face as I thought of our class trip to Washington, D.C. in tenth grade. Me, Laura and our friends had all been so excited to plan every detail. We knew who was rooming with who and which boys we'd try to sneak into our rooms. Of course, Ryan, Eddie and our other guy friends were hatching similar plans. Everything finally came together when we all agreed to sneak down to the hotel pool on our last night. Everyone had a blast hanging out with each other. Man, those were some good times.

Back when we were the same height.
And that scrunchie was still a hit.

I sighed and passed that time off as silly kid's play, reminding myself that I was an adult now. Those were simpler times. Now I was forced to make tough choices about everything that mattered in my life like traveling, school and love.

I remembered Ryan's email, and Elisha's interpretation of it. The more I thought about it, the more I felt that this time Elisha was wrong. After all these years, it was stupid to think Ryan cared what I did in Europe or otherwise. To think he would write me that email because he still had feelings for me was ridiculous. He was probably still with Natasha, and if not her, then some other lucky girl. He was living the college life and he certainly wasn't pining over someone from his past. And neither was I.

Carrying my large backpack, I filed off the boat and found the orange lamppost we had agreed to meet under (it was the only one I could find, so I figured it was the right one). I set my backpack down and tried to look cool. I had no choice but to believe he would meet me here.

Suddenly, I heard a voice shout my name and I was instantly relieved. I scanned the crowd, searching for those blue eyes. Just then, I felt hands on my hips, and I spun around to see his smiling face.

I knew I made the right decision.

AUGUST 18, 2002, 18 YEAR- OLD (SEVERAL MONTHS LATER)
#LovesLaborsLost

"But I love you."

"I don't tink ya do, Rana."

"How would you know what I feel?"

"Love is just- "

"Stop it! Stop with the 'illusion' talk, Paul. I can't take it anymore," I exclaimed.

I plopped down on our bed feeling defeated. Tears were starting to fall.

He put on his work trousers and sat down on the other side of the bed. I was sure he was tired of having the same conversation over and over again.

Ever since he had brought me back to Ireland, things hadn't been the same between us. We only stayed in Mallorca for a few weeks before Paul thought it made more sense to head back to Ireland and get a real job. I had agreed, it was the most logical step. He already had a position lined up and seemed to have a plan in place: we could move to the city and get our own apartment. He knew someone who would put me to work as a waitress under the table.

Paul had taken care of me the second I stepped off that boat. He literally peeled my bananas before handing them to me and made sure my seatbelt was fastened on the plane. I even listened as he called his mother and told her he'd be bringing the "most special person" in his life home and he couldn't wait for her to meet me.

But back in a familiar setting, surrounded by his family and friends, things changed. He wasn't the carefree Paul I fell in love with months earlier. He now felt obligated to take care of both of us and it weighed on him. I missed those days in Spain and Amsterdam, where we were carefree. I had been desperately trying to get back to that place. But I came to realize that Paul wasn't able to.

When we first arrived in Limerick we moved in with his mother for a few weeks so Paul could find the perfect place for us. This quickly went awry when Paul's mother started complaining about how her very Catholic neighbors were gossiping about the American bimbo Paul had brought home from Spain (me!).

Thankfully, we moved out pretty quickly and settled into our own apartment. We talked about only staying in Ireland for a few months before heading to the U.S. Paul was really excited to visit, and I was ecstatic to introduce him to everyone back home.

Who knew, maybe we'd make our way down to South America eventually, and then on to Australia, and wherever else we wanted to go. The world was our oyster and we would travel it together.

But the way things were going lately, I wasn't sure our plan was going to work out. Paul wouldn't say "I love you," something that, after living with him for five months, I not only wanted to hear, I *needed* to hear.

"Why's eet so important that I say it to ya?"

"Because it is, Paul. I need to know that we're on the same page. I'm getting the feeling you...like don't have feelings for me anymore or something," I said, now silently crying.

We sat there in silence and I waited for him to touch me, hold me, put his hand on mine... but it never came.

221

"Yeah. Maybe you're right, Rana," he said softly.

I wanted to crawl into the closet and sob. I looked at Paul who couldn't do anything but gaze at the floor. I stood up and walked out of our bedroom, into the hallway and out the door of our tiny apartment onto the chilly streets of Limerick. I had no idea where I was headed or what I was doing.

As I moped along the brick roads I couldn't help but notice the old sewer grates that were strategically placed every fifty feet or so. Why hadn't I noticed these before?

Suddenly, I stopped. It was his last name clear as day. Cavanaugh, maybe spelled slightly differently, but it was the same. And for the first time in a long time I thought of Ryan.

Real sewer lids in Ireland

Despite the cold, a warm and familiar feeling started to flow through my body. Ryan never had a problem saying "I love you." How odd that I was now pining for Paul to love me the way that Ryan once had.

Exhausted, I hopped over the sewer lids and kept walking.

That night, I dreamt about Ryan, and a week later I finally left Ireland behind. It was time to go and my visa was about to expire, so unless Paul and I wanted to make a bigger commitment, I was going to be forced out.

It had been one hell of a journey, but I wasn't sure if I was ready to go back. I had learned more about myself than I could have ever imagined; I was stronger than I thought, I had real courage and I realized that putting everything on the line for someone else was sometimes worth it and sometimes not.

And the jury's still out on this one.

AUGUST 28, 2002, 18 YEARS-OLD
#LifeGoesOn

I could barely get out of bed. The weight of everything was almost too much to bear. I slept, watched tons of TV, and moped around every day. I was officially depressed.

I had no idea what I had to look forward to now or what I was going to do. Everything back home seemed so...subpar. And, as my loving parents reminded me every day since I'd been back, I had to get a job.

It was over with Paul the minute I got on that plane, but I hated admitting it. He had offered me so much: travel, adventure, excitement, hope. Now all of that had vanished. I felt homesick for a place that I couldn't even define.

My family was happy to see me again, but they could not get used to my new Irish accent. It wasn't until I was back home that I realized I had acquired one.

I reflected on the day I must have officially picked it up. Paul's friend, Debbie came over to visit us in our apartment. I liked Debbie. She was an art teacher and full of life, like a lot of Irish gals.

As she sat across from me chatting about work, I suddenly couldn't hear her accent anymore. It had vanished. I tried to concentrate really hard on listening for it but it just wasn't there. It only took a few months, but I guess that's the day I truly assimilated.

Back home, when my family first heard me say, "ya know what I mean, like?" they stared at me in bewilderment. They were definitely in culture shock, and so was I.

"Rana? You awake?" I heard my dad say through the door.

I looked at my clock: 11:32. I had only slept for about five hours.

"Yeah," I sighed. I was not ready for the talk he promised me we'd have in person. If he wanted to lecture me on how irresponsible I had been, now just wasn't the time.

He opened my door and put some folded laundry on my desk. Ever since retirement he had taken on many of the household chores since my mom was still working.

"How ya feelin'?" he asked standing over me.

I laid still, my covers pulled up to my chin, facing away from him. I stared at the Janis Joplin poster on my wall, wanting to disappear into it.

"Fine."

"Well then get outta bed. Come to the store with me. I gotta go grocery shopping, and I don't know what you like anymore now that you're all European with an accent," he poked me. Very typical of him to make a joke to break the ice.

"No, Dad. I don't feel like it."

"Come on, let's get out of here. I'll let you drive. I bet you haven't driven in eight months. It'll be, how do you say, 'grand?'" he mocked me with his best Irish accent.

Driving made me think of when Paul tried to teach me how to operate a stick shift on a country road in Limerick, on the opposite side of the street to boot. We had laughed (and tried not to panic) as I burned up his mom's gearshift. The memory gave me shooting pains in my stomach. I cringed.

"I can't, Dad. I'm not even dressed. I haven't brushed my teeth or anything," I whined, trying to make excuses.

"You mean since you've been back?" he quipped.

"Dad!"

"I'll be downstairs. I'm leaving in twenty minutes. And you're coming," he said ripping off my covers.

I didn't put up a fight. As he shut the door behind him, I headed to my closet to find an outfit. I felt a chill as I stepped out into the morning air from under my covers.

As I gazed into my closet everything felt so un-European. I had totally changed the way I dressed and my old wardrobe didn't reflect the 'new me.' It lacked something.

After finding a pair of wide-legged jeans and a white top, I headed downstairs waiting to be ridiculed; my dad was going to say something about the way I looked, I just knew it.

Much to my surprise, he didn't.

As we hopped in the car I felt bad about underestimating him. He could be very sensitive when he wanted to be, and he obviously could see that I was hurting right now.

"So, what did it look like?" my dad asked handing me the keys.

Confused, I asked, "What? What did what look like?"

"The train that hit you."

Annnnnd, there it was. I spoke too soon. Welcome home, Rana.

AUGUST 29, 2002, 18 YEARS-OLD
#BlastFromThePast

"Seriously, it's time to get out of the house," my sister, Antonia said.

"I've been getting out," I defensively stated.

"The drug store doesn't count. I'm with Tonia, you're coming out with us tonight. My friend's band is playing a show. It'll be fun," Elisha piped in.

"But I can't get in. I'm not old enough, remember?" I groaned.

"Problem solved. I have my friend Gabby's I.D. for you," Antonia replied as she slapped it down on the kitchen table.

"Quieter," Elisha nodded towards our parents watching TV in the living room.

I picked up the driver's license, "She looks nothing like me," I retorted handing Antonia the card.

I knew Gabby. Gabby was Hawaiian and she had very dark skin and jet-black hair. She was also about fifty pounds heavier than me. This wasn't a vanity thing, I just didn't want to get caught.

"It won't matter, Elisha knows the guy who's checking I.D.'s at the door," Antonia answered.

"Guys, I don't know..."

"Listen, all you've been doing is sulking about Paul. Now I know these past few weeks have been tough, but you're going to have fun tonight. It's time you loosen up and forget about him for a while," Elisha agreed.

"Pleeeeeeeeeease?" they both sang in unison.

As nervous as I was, the guy at the door hardly even looked at 'my' I.D. Thank God because I really wasn't up for getting arrested. But now that we were here, I was glad I came.

It was a packed house and, thus, hot and stuffy. Antonia had let me borrow a shirt she just bought, something that was practically unheard of so I knew she must *really* be feeling sorry for me. I took full advantage of the situation and talked her into letting me borrow some of her hoop earrings as well. I was also hoping not to run into anyone I knew, if I did, I was liable to break into tears if they asked me anything about my trip. Just in case, I thought I'd say that the reason I went to Europe was to study fashion for a semester and leave it at that.

On the way back from the restroom, I heard my name, "Rana! How are you?! It's been so long!" I turned around and saw Ryan's mom coming toward me, reaching for a hug?

"Kelly, ohmygosh, I'm good. How have you been?" I asked trying to match her enthusiasm.

"I'm great! You look fabulous. What's new in your life?! Wait, how did you get in here...? Never mind, you don't have to tell me!" Kelly responded.

I couldn't remember the last time I had seen her—high school? She always seemed to like me, and I always thought she was great. She still looked perfectly polished, her hair and makeup were exquisite and her clothes were trendy, unlike most moms her age.

Of course, seeing her made me think of Ryan. I had thought about responding to his email a million times as I tried to sort out all this Paul stuff. But I hadn't known what to say, and I didn't want to get into the reasons why I had stayed away so long. Ryan was the last person I wanted to talk to about Paul.

Plus, I was afraid he had a girlfriend, or worse, that he was still with Natasha.

I smiled and thanked her for not ratting me out. "Nothing much, just got back from Europe."

"Europe?! That's wonderful, I always knew you'd go places!" Kelly shouted over the band.

Should I try to give her a signal that I missed Ryan? That I got on a plane home right after I dreamt about him?

"Thank you, that's so nice of you to say. Are you guys visiting family in town?"

"Well the girls and I actually just moved back a few months ago. I ran into your mom the other day, she is too sweet!" she said changing the subject.

'Me and the girls?' OMG Ryan's parents got a divorce, my parents must have known, but forgot to tell me.

I looked around to see who Kelly had come in with and I spotted four ladies around her age. All of them were blonde, pretty and elegant. Bingo.

"Yes, she's somethin' else," I smiled. "Soooo Ryan moved back, too?" I boldly asked.

"No, he's still in school at BG."

"And how's he doing?" And does he have a girlfriend?

"He's doing really well! He's working part-time while he finishes school. Studying early childhood education," she said taking a sip from the drink she was holding.

"I remember. Does he know what grade yet?"

"First grade!" she said beaming with pride. "Ya know, I had your framed picture in our basement for years," Kelly continued as she took a seat at the bar. I followed suit.

"Really!?" my curiosity was now piqued. I liked the idea that any girlfriend Ryan had brought home would have seen that picture and felt slightly insecure that there was another girl Ryan might have liked better. "Which picture?"

"Some picture you gave Ryan when you guys were younger, I don't know. I just thought it was too cute to throw out." Her phone buzzed in her purse and she reached in to look at it. I thought about what photo it could be, maybe my 7th grade school picture?

If this cheesy grin couldn't intimidate a grown woman,
I don't know what could.

"Any who, what was I saying?"

"You have a picture of me..."

"Right! The picture, it's just darling. You were my favorite of Ryan's girlfriends. I always thought you two would end up together. But I guess not," she said reaching for the pretzel bowl.

I was her 'favorite,' was all I heard. I was too distracted to respond.

"So, wow, Rana, what a blast from the past, huh?! Cheers!" she announced holding her drink up.

"Whoa. Freaky. Do you think he's like... your soul mate or something?" Laura asked the next morning over coffee. The night before I'd had another dream about Ryan. It was different from the one I had when I was with Paul, but still it threw me.

I paused. Everything inside of me wanted the answer to be 'yes,' but it sounded too good to be true. Finding your true love when you were nine years old just wasn't something that happened to people.

Did I even believe that there was one person out there for everyone? Laura hadn't said anything that I hadn't already thought many times before—were Ryan and I truly destined to be with each other?

"Nah, it was just a stupid dream. I probably had it because I saw his mom. That's all." I replied.

"Yeah but this isn't the first time, Rana."

"People have dreams about other people all the time and it doesn't mean anything. I'm not special." I replied brushing her off. "Besides, what would I even do, call him? 'Oh, hi Ryan, it's Rana. I have hot dreams about you every night. Will you marry me?'" I said sarcastically.

"I bet you still know his number by heart." Laura mused.

9-6-6-2-8-3-7. "Yeah right."

"Just teasin.'"

"Hilarious, Lor."

"Look, I'm all for anything that will get you through this Paul thing. Even if it means Ryan Cavanaugh. Did I just say that?"

"You did," I took a sip from my enormous mug of coffee—so much better than tea.

"There must be something wrong with me today," she quipped.

"Hey let's call Derek and we can all have a reunion," I joked.

"Ew. Let's not get carried away. You're right, let's just let the past be the past." Laura had broken up with Derek the summer after senior year, and she was totally over him.

"Exactly."

"I better get going. Gotta study for my stupid chem test. Love ya!"

"OK, call me," I waved.

What I didn't tell Laura was that I had already analyzed my dream about Ryan. And I was confident I knew what it all meant, but why was this happening now?

I had dreamt that Ryan and I were hanging out on a houseboat. Anthony Lucarelli was there and he was acting obnoxious. We couldn't wait for him to leave and when he finally did, we were all over each other.

I woke up, but when I fell back asleep, I had yet another dream about Ryan. This time we were at Powell. We were making out in an empty 3rd grade classroom. I left the room and saw Natasha wearing a formal gown talking on the phone down the hall. I hoped she wouldn't talk to me because I felt guilty for just kissing her boyfriend. Not only did she talk to me, she needed comforting because she was crying. I gave her a hug. Then I walked up the hall into a 1st grade classroom and sat down on the carpet with all the other kids, kinda like I was supposed to.

I had analyzed the dream using my dream dictionary and figured out that it probably meant Ryan represented one of the only boyfriends I ever had who was good enough for me. Someone who knew my worth and what I needed and deserved in a man.

AUGUST 10, 2004, 20 YEARS-OLD
#FollowYourDreams

After finishing most of my prerequisites at community college, I finally had the courage to leave Canton. I was accepted into the Fashion Design program at the Academy of Couture Art in Los Angeles.

I never would have had the guts to go if it wasn't for my European journey. That experience helped me to realize some crucial things about life and myself: that I was worth more than what some guy thought of me, that I'm capable of doing stuff on my own, that my family will always be there for me and that anything can happen. I was getting good at taking on things that scared me.

Ryan and I were both so busy with college we hardly saw one another. We never spoke about his last email to me. I kept tabs on him through mutual friends and knew he was doing well enough, which wasn't surprising.

Feeling like a new beginning was in order, I left behind everything I knew and stepped out on a limb. Again. And prayed to God that it would pay off.

PART IV

JANUARY 22, 2006, 22 YEARS-OLD
#ThisCantBeReal

"I feel like I just got kicked in the stomach," my brother, Joey said.

I started the car. I was numb and could barely focus on getting out of the parking garage. After nearly three weeks of parking here, you would think I would know my way out by now.

"Yeah, me too." I said holding back my tears.

"I mean I can't even believe it," he whispered as he gazed out the window.

Joey had never been the most talkative, but perhaps he needed to process everything out loud this time. Who could be themselves at a time like this?

"I can't either."

"Do you need me to drive?" he asked.

"No, I got it."

"OK..."

We rode in silence for the twenty-minute drive back to my parent's. I think I was still in shock. I still couldn't believe what happened over these last three weeks.

Less than a month ago, we finally convinced dad to go to the chiropractor after complaining that his back hurt and nothing seemed to help. Next thing we knew he was seeing an oncologist who told us he not only had lung cancer, but he was in stage four.

We prepared for many rounds of chemo and the whole family came together to discuss our options.

But dad went downhill, and fast. We all thought he had more time.

And tonight, at 11:01pm, as all five of us gathered around his hospital bed, he took his last breath.

My heart would never be the same. I was only twenty-two, too young to be father-less.

JANUARY 30, 2006, 22 YEARS-OLD
#IllBeThere

"Rana!" my mom called from downstairs.

"Yeah?" I yelled from my old bedroom. I'd been watching mindless TV to drown out my noisy grief.

I waited for her to respond. I could hear her talking on the phone—it rang? Was I in that much of a daze that I didn't even hear it? The funeral had been just days before, and my siblings and I decided that I'd be the one to stay in Ohio for an extra week to help my mom adjust. Not that anyone can adjust to being alone after thirty-three years of marriage.

Jeremy and I had only begun seeing each other so it was much too soon for him to come home with me. Besides, I couldn't think of a worse way to introduce a person to your family.

I walked out of my bedroom. "Ma, what'd you need?" I hollered down the stairs.

"Thank you, I really appreciate that," I heard her say into the phone.

"Hang on one second—Rana, the phones for you," she called up. I went back into my room and picked up the phone by my bed, "Hello?"

"Rana?"

239

"Hi," I would have recognized his raspy voice anywhere. My mom hung up the other line downstairs, and now I understood why she had been chatting when the call was really for me.

"Hey, it's Ryan."

"I know."

"Well I'm calling because...I read your dad's obituary in the paper. I mean, my mom did and she told me. I'm so sorry, Rana."

I wanted to cry. I could feel that familiar lump rising in my throat. "Yeah me too," I replied, my voice shaky.

"I just can't believe it," he said empathetically.

It was nice to hear from him. There weren't many people from my past who had reached out to share their condolences—and that had really disappointed me. I had expected to hear from Mary or some of my other high school girlfriends. I hadn't spoken to them in years, but I'm sure they had heard about my dad by now. Heck, I even wondered about Paul. I don't know how he would have found out across the ocean, but it just felt like he should have called or something.

When I mentioned how few of my old friends had gotten in touch, my mom told me that kind of thing took courage, so it didn't surprise me when I heard from Ryan, he was one of the bravest, kindest, and most thoughtful people I knew.

"I know, I can't believe it either," I replied sliding down the side of my bed to the floor. I felt so defeated.

"He was such a nice guy." Ryan took a beat and then added, "Scary, but nice."

I laughed. I appreciated his attempt to lighten the mood. It's okay to smile, I reminded myself yet again.

"Yeah, he can be scary. *Could* be, I mean..." my voice trailed off when I recognized my mistake.

240

"Hey remember that time Doug and I rode our bikes to your house in sixth grade? And your dad was washing the car in your driveway and you were playing in the garage. We asked if you were home, because we could see you plain as day, but your dad insisted you weren't there!"

"Yeah! Ohmygosh, you guys were all like, 'but she's right there' and he was like, 'I said she's not home!'"

"We ran our bikes away so fast," we both shared a laugh.

I had forgotten all about that. It was so nice to picture him in a way that didn't involve hospitals, cancer or dying.

Ryan and I hadn't spoken in years but that didn't seem to matter. Time was never an issue with us. We had a friendship and a connection that time just couldn't touch.

When most people spoke to me after my dad passed, they handled me like I was fragile, about to break at any moment. It wasn't their fault, it's hard to know how to respond. But this felt good to just share stories about my dad, who he was and what he was like.

Talking to Ryan reminded me of my dad's funeral. Because he always made us laugh, we decided that instead of a serious ceremony we would have people share their funny memories of him. I loved listening to my dad's friends recall laugh-out-loud stories from work, many of which I never knew had happened. I talked about my return home from Europe when I looked so horrible that he asked me about the train that hit me. Ryan's story would have fit in perfectly.

"Tell me, how are you doing?"

It was a question I had been asked a million times in the last couple of weeks. But hearing it from Ryan made me start to silently sob. I put the phone down to catch my breath.

"Rana, are you there?"

"Sorry...yes," I replied trying to regain my composure.

"Oh man, Rana...This is awful. I can't imagine what you're going through so I won't pretend I do."

"Thank you. It means a lot that you called."

"Of course."

We sat in silence.

"Hey Rana? I hope you know that I'm always here for you."

I took a moment to reflect, "I do."

And it was the truth—I knew that out of everyone, I could always count on Ryan.

♥ GROWN UP US – DECEMBER 30, 2008 ♥
#BreakingUpIsHardToDo

"I just don't think this is going to work. I'm sorry." I finally said.

"What?"

I'd been dreading this day for weeks. It was never easy to let someone down. I hated it. I ran everything I was going to say past Jason earlier this afternoon. He told me to keep it short and simple, not to go in circles and give a million excuses she would see right through—just get right to the point.

"Look, it's nothing you did or didn't do. It's just...I guess I don't feel enough chemistry between us," I hesitated.

"Wow, I'm shocked. I don't even know what to say."

"I'm really sorry," I said emphatically.

"How was I reading this all wrong? I thought we were doing great," she sputtered, trying to make sense of what I was saying.

It made me wince.

"Just be honest with me, is there someone else?"

Huh? How did she know that? Panic began to rise in my throat; I was officially cornered. But I didn't want to lie even though Jason told me under no circumstance to admit it.

"Don't worry, your deer in headlights look says everything," she said giving me attitude.

"It's not like that..."

"Who is she? Do I know her?" She turned to face me on the couch. Guess I wasn't going to get off that easy.

"No," I said looking her in the eye. She seemed to be on the verge of crying and I was beginning to feel like an even bigger douche.

"What's her name?" she scooted a little further from me creating more distance between us.

"April, don't do this, I don't want to…"

"Tell me! I have a right to know, Ryan," April demanded, her face turning pink.

I stood up and walked over to the mantle to give us both some space. I was startled by her reaction—not that her anger wasn't warranted—it was just that I'd never seen this side of her.

"Well?"

"Rana. Her name is Rana," I let out a sigh. It was the first time I admitted this out loud. It still felt surreal that me and Rana might get back together after all this time. That is, if she'd still have me.

"And who is this Rana? Did you meet her while I was visiting my parents?" April asked.

Her long auburn hair almost reached her waist. Tonight, she was a little more dressed up than usual with a sequin sweater and black leggings. She probably thought out reunion was going to be…not this.

I clearly hadn't been planning the same type of evening, I was wearing some old jeans and a Cleveland Cavaliers t-shirt.

"No, no, it's not like that at all. We've known each other since fourth grade. She's recently come back into my life, and I realized that I have feelings for her. Some unresolved ones, I guess."

I wasn't sure how April was processing all of this, and I was on edge knowing that some women can go from zero to sixty in two seconds flat. And she seemed like she was teetering on the edge. I chose my words wisely.

"You've talked about women from your past, how come you never mentioned her?" April quizzed. She flipped her hair to her other shoulder, looking skeptical.

"There was never any reason to. She lives in L.A. and we only reconnected over the holidays. I don't even know if there's anything real between us anymore. But it's unfair to be in relationship with you while I'm still figuring out all this stuff with Rana. It would be like lying to you. I hate doing this, I think you're an awesome girl. And we both know you deserve better."

She looked down at the floor but didn't respond.

I tried to analyze her silence.

"April, I never meant to hurt you," I said cautiously walking over and putting my hand on her shoulder.

She stood up and met my gaze, "I know."

"Are you OK?"

"I will be," she gave me a half smile. I was relieved we weren't going to end this with a screaming match.

"Look, it's probably best that I just go. There's really nothing more to say. I'm just going to use your bathroom and then I'll get outta here," she said.

"Sure, no prob," I said stepping out of her way.

I may not be a genius when it came to women (as Jason was always quick to point out). But I knew I had done well here—April was upset, but she also understood. And I could bet right now she was retrieving her overnight bag from underneath my sink.

♥ GROWN UP US – DECEMBER 31, 2008 ♥
#GiveLoveAChance

I stood in the corner waiting for the barista to call my name. From here I had a perfect view of the door, so I'd see her the second she walked in.

I looked at my phone, "10:03," I said aloud.

So, she was three minutes late—not a big deal, I thought, trying to calm my anxiety.

She hadn't sounded overly enthusiastic when I suggested we meet for coffee. I even drove the hour from Cleveland to Canton to make it easier for her. After grabbing my latte, I snagged a table and tried not to stare at the door.

My phone read 10:12 when she burst into the café, bringing a rush of cold air with her. She looked incredible, which made me even more nervous. Her hair was long and wavy, and she wore brown leather gloves and tall boots. She was stunning. And in a small town like this she immediately stood out. I could see now more than ever that she was always going to be bigger than Canton—she belonged in a major city, like L.A. It suited her much better than here, although I hated to admit it. Big cities had a way of swallowing you up. But I couldn't imagine that happening to Rana.

I waved to get her attention.

She saw me and briskly walked to the table, "Sorry I'm late."

I stood up to hug her, "You're fine. What can I get you to drink, a soy latte, right?"

She smirked. "A soy latte would be fine. Thanks," she said unwrapping her scarf and taking off her coat.

I went over to order as she sat down and came back to the table with her latte. I had a flashback to the week before when I brought her a latte in my bed. A lot had changed since then. "Thanks for coming," I stated as I took my seat across from her.

"Sure. You said you wanted to talk, so I'm willing to listen," she replied.

"Right. Well I know I didn't get back to you the other day after you told me how you felt about us..."

"Uh-huh," she said looking blankly at me.

That's fair. I expected a touch of bitterness. "I just wanted to tell you, first, how sorry I am. I know that probably seemed... insensitive."

"That's one way to put it," she said blowing on her latte.

It made me chuckle, "I deserve that, Rana. But I should be honest with you, the idea of a long-distance relationship kind of makes me-"

"Scared." I guess it was sort of obvious. I wasn't fooling anyone.

"Yeah. I think it makes me nervous being all the way in Ohio when you're in L.A. And you've got this really cool job working in Hollywood with all of those actors and celebrity types... where do I truly fit into all of that?"

"Ryan, I'm still the same person I've always been. My job is cool and all, but it's just what I do it's not who I am. Working in fashion makes me happy, but at the end of the day if I don't have anyone to share it with then, what's the point?"

I sighed, "I saw my parents fall apart because of too much distance. I know most couples can't survive that sort of thing," I explained.

"I understand."

"Long distance is hard."

"Look, did you want me to come here so you could tell me face to face why this won't work? Because I already got the hint when you didn't text me back."

"What if you work on a movie with Robert Downey Jr and fall in love? I heard he's very charming!" I joked.

I saw her crack a smile and finally relax enough to sit back in her chair. Arms folded, "Shut up." I could always make her laugh (or at least smile) when she was angry. And it was something I took great pride in.

"Seriously Ryan, what do you want from me?"

♥ GROWN UP US – DECEMBER 31, 2008 ♥
#TheBestIsYetToCome

I'd been wondering what Ryan wanted ever since our chance meeting when I was home for Thanksgiving last month.

Annabelle and Gia had convinced me to go out on one of the biggest drinking nights of the year: the night before Thanksgiving. When I walked in the bar, I froze dead in my tracks when I spotted him. It had been years since we'd seen each other and he was...well, a man. He had a full beard and his biceps were even fuller. He looked straight out of *GQ* with his tight electric blue zip-up sweater. The scene felt like it was straight out of a Rom-Com—everything around us faded away as we locked eyes. Cliché, I know, but that's how it felt.

I don't remember seeing much of Annabelle and Gia after that, but I do remember walking right over to Ryan and insisting on buying him a drink—I just wanted to have him all to myself. So, we drank a little, we laughed and we really let loose for the first time...ever, really.

We all went to Doug's house after the bar closed and the night ended with the two of us dancing to "Banana Pancakes" while everyone else slept off the evening's adventures.

It couldn't have been any more romantic than if Ryan were chasing me through the airport to stop me before I got on my plane.

It felt like *finally* after all these years the timing might be right. But I tried to enjoy the moment and not put too much pressure on us.

We had vowed to stay in touch and kept good on our promise. Just minutes after I left he sent me a text. At first it was occasional, but as Christmas approached, it turned into nearly every day, and then several times a day. It was all harmless flirting and even though we agreed to hang out when I went back to Ohio for Christmas, it was still unclear whether it was purely platonic. For me? I sure didn't want it to be. And after our intense night of making-out a week ago, I was more convinced than ever that I wanted a real relationship with him. So, what were we doing here?

"Seriously Ryan, what do you want from me?" I asked.

He looked me in the eye and grabbed my hands, "Everything."

"Huh?"

"If you're in it, so am I. Let's try and make a go of this damn thing once and for all. Because, Rana, I've spent more than half of my life wondering whether we would ever really give this a try, and I don't want to do that anymore. I won't."

I smiled, totally caught off guard, "Really?"

"Yes, really! I've had my eye on you ever since Ms. Luciano's class. I know the goods when I see 'em," he winked.

"Ohmygosh!" I said throwing a sugar packet at him as we giggled.

He stood up and looped his finger into mine. The gesture was one I forgot all about. It was touching. He pulled me close and kissed me. He didn't care who was watching.

I pulled away, my mind reeling with questions, "Wait, how is this going to work?"

"I have no idea. But we'll find a way. We've always found a way to stay in each other's lives—this time it will just be a real commitment."

And that was good enough for me.

♥ GROWN UP US – THE DAY BEFORE THANKSGIVING 2009 ♥
#CatchingACurveball

"You're sure you can't come pick me up?" I asked.

"I wish I could, but I'm so busy with work. I really need to catch up because we don't have school for the rest of the week. I'll see you right afterwards, I promise."

I sighed into the phone as I tried to hide my disappointment. My flight from L.A. to Cleveland was going to land in about four hours and this was the first time we'd see each other in months. But I'd waited this long, what's another few hours?

"Don't worry, Doug will be there to pick you up. He'll take you to your mom's house and I'll meet you down there," Ryan explained.

"OK," I said.

"Don't worry, baby. The good news is that we're going to see each other today."

He made a good point; the important thing was that I was coming home. It didn't matter who was picking me up.

"Yeah, you're right," I admitted.

Long distance was like Ryan predicted: hard. Inevitably, we had our ups and downs, but we promised to see each other once every eight weeks. Ryan had come out to L.A. for almost the entire summer as soon as school let out. And although it was my busy season at

work, he was patient and understanding. He was always home waiting for me with dinner ready, even if it was after midnight (which it
often was). I was thrilled at the fact that Ryan and I would be spending a lot more time together in the coming year—in about a month
he was moving to L.A. to be with me.

I reflected on the past twelve months. It was so surreal that now,
nearly a year after it had all begun, I was heading home for Thanksgiving. Again. But this time I'd be going home to my childhood
sweetheart. If there's one thing I'd learned over the last twenty-five
years, it was that life definitely throws curve balls.

When my plane landed in Cleveland, I immediately turned my
phone on to see if Ryan had gotten in touch. I smiled as I listened to
a voicemail from him saying how excited he was to see me. I was
thrilled at the thought of spending our first Thanksgiving together.
We had a lot to look forward to this weekend.

Doug picked me up at the airport and filled me in on what was
new in his life as we rode along I-77 to Canton. We also discussed
the details of the surprise going-away party I was throwing for Ryan
before he moved out to L.A. next month. It was something I'd been
planning for a while and was confident I could actually keep it a
secret.

"One quick thing, Rana: do you care if we stop at Powell? I
promise it'll be fast. I dropped off my resume last week and told
them I'd stop in today to check on it," Doug explained.

"Powell Elementary? Like where we went to elementary school?
He nodded.

"Geez, I haven't been there in years," I said.

Doug had just gotten his teaching license and I knew he had
been looking for an elementary school job.

"I know, right? It's so weird I might actually work there."

We approached Powell and I realized I hadn't been there since my last day of 5th grade. I quickly calculated that fifteen years had gone by. Ick, that made me feel old.

Doug pulled around to the side of the building where the double doors let kids out every day.

"Ha! This is right where the buses used to wait, remember?" I exclaimed.

"Yep," he said with a smirk that made me raise a brow.

He parked right in front of the doors. I sat reflecting, waiting for Doug to get out of the car and head inside.

Then, something happened. Was that Ryan walking out of the building?

I looked at Doug who nudged me to get out of the car, "Go on."

Wait, is this what I think it is?

I ran over to Ryan and hugged him. I could smell his familiar zesty cologne. He embraced me then reached down and took my hands. His were sweaty and a bit shaky.

He was dressed in jeans and a nice sweater, reminiscent of what he wore the night we reconnected almost a year ago.

"Ryan?"

"Rana Mancini, I've loved you practically my whole life," he went down to one knee.

"Ohmygod..." I began to shake. I looked around and saw several teachers and students gazing out of the windows with excited looks on their faces.

"I want to ask you..." he pulled out a box from his back pocket.

I stood there in silence and felt tears start to stream down my face.

He continued, his voice cracking and tears welling up in his eyes, "Rana, will you marry me?"

I stared at him in disbelief and forgot I was supposed to actually respond, my emotions running too high to think clearly.

It reminded me of that time so many years ago when he casually asked me to be his girlfriend on the way to the bus—right here, in nearly this very spot. Who knew that one moment would change the course of my life?

"Yes, yes!" I gasped.

He stood up to wipe a tear from my cheek and slipped the ring on my finger. I gazed into his eyes, still in shock. It was the first time I had ever seen him cry.

Our onlookers let out a cheer, and I let out a nervous giggle. Through one of the windows, Ms. Luciano waved with a grin.

Ryan put his hands on my cheeks and kissed me in the same spot he had first kissed me that day in fifth grade.

This was one curveball I would happily catch.

Thankfully, someone who worked for the school was nice enough to hide in the bushes and grab some photos (this was before you hired professional photographers to capture it!).

♥ GROWN UP US – DECEMBER 17, 2009 ♥
#TBT

I was exhausted when I arrived at LaGuardia Airport. I had just finished shooting a horror film less than two days before and working seventy hours a week on set had started to catch up with me. I was relieved that, after this last trip, I would be off until mid-January.

I'd only be in New York for a few days. Leaving Ryan back in L.A. when he had just moved there wasn't ideal, but I couldn't pass up this opportunity, and he of course, was supportive. He was already lining up interviews of his own at local elementary schools.

Tomorrow evening could change everything. I was about to meet with potential investors for my very own fashion line, meaning my dream career was finally within reach.

Arriving at my hotel, I quickly fell onto the bed and passed out. I loved New York, and was thrilled to be there, but this trip was all work and I needed my rest.

The next day, in an effort to distract myself from my looming dinner that evening, I decided to head to Chinatown for some authentic Pho. Soup soothed me when I was stressed out. I'd spent the morning doing my best to memorize my pitch and anticipate any questions, and now I just needed to relax and calm down.

I stepped out of the cab and the freezing air made my lungs burn. I quickly put on my gloves and wrapped my oversized scarf tighter.

I looked above the sea of pedestrians to try and catch a glimpse of an authentic Vietnamese restaurant—in other words, one that real New Yorkers knew about, not tourists.

I was walking up a hill when I heard my name. I recognized the voice immediately and turned to face him.

"Rana? Gosh, is that reely you, like?"

He gave me a hug and I'm not sure if I hugged him back. I was beyond astonished.

"What are ya doin' here? Ya live here, do ya?"

"Wow. I can't believe it..." I stammered.

He wore a black blazer and stylish jeans. His hair was short and his eyes a bright blue, just like I remembered.

"This is so strange, wouldn't ya say?!" he exclaimed.

"Yeah Paul, it really is. Um, I'm here on business, I actually live in L.A.," I said trying to remember what he was asking me. I flashed back momentarily to Amsterdam, Mallorca, Limerick—all those experiences now seemed like a lifetime ago. So much had changed.

"That's cool, I'm here on business, too. What are dee odds of runnin' into each utter here and now, huh?"

"I'd say the odds are pretty damn small," I let out a chuckle. He followed suit.

"Well you look amazin," he said with that twinkle in his eye.

At first I was surprised at how forward he was, but then I remembered he had always been forthcoming, even when it hurt.

I adore him. But (+ there's often a BUT) my mind is telling me that I deserve more. He won't tell me he loves me. I know they're just words, but he doesn't believe in law. He used to .... and I think he's lost feelings for me. I know he has, he said so.

An excerpt from the actual journal that I kept in Ireland.

Judging by his lack of a ring, I guessed he was still single. And if I weren't wearing gloves he would have seen I was engaged.

"Thank you, Paul." You're damn straight I look amazing.

"May I ask what kind of business ya've got here?"

"Fashion. I'm finally designing my own line," I said proudly. There was no sweeter revenge than success, and I was so grateful for the chance to tell him how well I was doing face-to-face.

"Of course, ya are. You were always a go-getter. I'm not surprised at all," he replied.

Good answer.

"Thanks," I said straightening up. "And what about you, what are you doing in New York?"

"I'm an architect so I've been sent out to put dee finishing touches on a project I helped head up," he grabbed my arm and gently swung me around. "There, you see dat one? Dat one's mine," he said proudly as his cheek grazed mine. I was quickly reminded of how touchy-feely he could be.

He let me go, turned and looked me in the eye letting it all sink in, "Rana, is this really happenin' like? I can't believe I've run into ya halfway across da world after all dees years. It's mint to be, maybe?"

"Funny, I feel like you've said that very thing before," I replied. Ha! Take that.

His face was grave. Was that remorse? Sorrow? Perhaps even regret?

"Have dinner wit me tomorrow- will you still be in town?"

"Whoa, what?"

"Please. Let me show ya how much I've grown up, like. Back when ya knew me I was a little boy. And I'd like to get to know ya again. This time as a man," he boldly confessed.

It almost sounded rehearsed as if he had imagined what he'd say to me if he ever got the chance. I had imagined a similar situation, but my speech was a little more about 'how do you like me now?' not 'take me back.'

And the rules definitely made clear that whenever you run into an ex you should always, always, always (did I mention always?) make them feel like they lost. And I mean *really* feel it. Because let's face it, it's *always* their loss.

"Oh. I don't think that- "

"Say yes. Or how about da coffee? Or tae? We'll go to a place that has both so no pressure hare. Come on, for old time's sake, like," he winked.

I studied his chiseled face. It seemed genuine enough and I could see a hint of desperation that gave me extreme satisfaction. And if I was honest, I wanted to hear him out. Maybe have him tell me he had been an idiot and made a huge mistake seven years ago. And could one deny that there would naturally be some unfinished business between two people who were once international lovers? "All right. When and where?"

He smiled. Relieved. "Awesome. Dare's a little place in Soho, called Flagship. Tomorrow, 7:00?"

"I'll be there," I nodded.

"Fantastic, lass! Look, I gotta go, I'm late for a meetin,'" he said giving me another hug, this time squeezing a little tighter. "I can't wait- reelly, lass. I've missed ya," he said giving me a kiss on the cheek.

I watched him disappear into the crowd of people. I put my hand where he kissed my cheek and couldn't believe Paul had just walked back into my life.

That evening, I put everything aside and had an incredible meeting with my potential investors. As nervous as I was, I felt calm and collected as I showed off my colorful samples, displayed the drawings for my women's casual wear line and forecasted next season's trends. By the time I left, I truly felt it was a match made in career heaven.

My dream had always been to work for myself and design my own line. And it was finally coming into fruition. I was on cloud nine.

♥ GROWN UP US – THE FOLLOWING EVENING ♥
#OTP

Lipstick: check.

New pantsuit from my own collection: check.

Killer heels I had bought that morning: check.

I took one final look in the mirror and I was pleased. I wanted to make sure I looked my best when I saw him again.

I was running about ten minutes behind schedule, in true form, I was fashionably late.

After the airport shuttle dropped me off, I found the United Airlines counter and explained my situation to the agent. Leaving a day earlier than my scheduled departure was going to be the ultimate surprise for Ryan. After all, my business was officially over here; I had done what I came to do. And now there was nothing I wanted more than to be home with him anticipating the holidays. And our new life together. Paul was going to be in for a surprise when I didn't show up for dinner, but I had decided against taking an evening to stroll back through the past. Ryan was my future. Paul represented a different time, a time that was over for me.

"Hi babe!" I shouted walking in the door with my luggage.

"Hey! What the heck are you doing here?!" Ryan exclaimed, jumping off the couch. He gave me a kiss and took the suitcase out of my hands.

"I wanted to surprise you!" I said giving him a huge hug. "Are you surprised?"

"Yes! I'm so glad you're back," he said holding me tight. I let him embrace me as I closed my eyes to breathe him in. "You look great, by the way."

"Thanks." I smiled to myself. "So, how'd your interview go?" I said muffled into his chest.

"It went great, I just heard this afternoon that I got the job! I start right after Christmas break. But enough about me, how did the meeting go?" he said pulling me back to look into my eyes.

We plopped onto the couch, and I told him everything; how the investors were impressed with my samples and how my drive and attitude were exactly what they were looking for in a partner. My studio would still be in L.A. and we'd conduct virtual meetings on a weekly basis. Fortunately for us, I'd just travel to New York when I needed to. We had a shared vision of seeing a collection of mine at New York Fashion Week in the following year.

"You're amazing! I told you they'd love you," he said.

"Thank you for believing in me. I can't wait to marry you."

"I'm the lucky one," he said stroking my hair. "Speaking of, have you given anymore thought to setting a date?"

"Actually, I have. I was thinking New Year's Eve, next year."

"Oh yeah?" his said, sounding curious.

"Yeah, I like that it's the end and the beginning of something all at the same time. And next year it falls on a Friday, which is perfect," I said.

"I like it," he beamed.

"Me too. Soooooo, do we have a date?"

"Yep. I'll meet you there. New Year's Eve," he said kissing me again. My stomach did flip flops.

I was giddy with excitement as I thought about a day in time that would always belong to us. December 31, 2010. Our day.

"Perfect. So how did everything go while I was away?" I asked.

"Good. Talked to the realtor again and she said she has some listings to show us next week."

"Really? Sweet."

We knew we couldn't stay in my small apartment forever. My lease had just ended and I was living month to month. Besides, we needed a fresh start and purchasing a home together was one step in that direction.

"Next year is going to be a big one for us. New jobs, a new house...a wedding," I smirked.

"This wedding is going to be huge, isn't it?" he asked.

"Not as huge as my dress, but yeah," I winked.

He shook his head and laughed, "I can only imagine." He continued, "So what else did you do in New York besides impress the hell out of some millionaires?"

This was my chance to tell him about Paul. To come clean and say that I not only saw Paul, but I agreed to have dinner with him, too. I briefly thought of Paul sitting alone in the restaurant, waiting, me never showing up. I felt a twinge of guilt, but I had made the right decision—I had no business rehashing anything with some guy I used to date.

I looped his finger into mine and decided I didn't need to ruin this beautiful moment talking about some past ex. I was moving forward with Ryan, not looking back.

In the end, I truly wanted 'the nice guy.' The guy who had always loved me and the guy who was always with me, even when we were apart.

"Nothing much, pretty uneventful," I said as I crawled up to him and hugged his neck.

"Well, next time I wanna go with," he said turning on the TV.

"Absolutely."

"Cause now that I have you, I don't want to leave your side."

"And I don't want you to," I said looping his finger into mine.

"I almost forgot, I found something when you were gone," he said. He got up and went into our bedroom. It was still girlie with its pink and green duvet and flower motif curtains. I had been slowly weeding out my pre-Ryan things, making way for the decor that was more 'us.'

"What is it?"

"I was moving some stuff around to make room for my boxes and I came across this," he said plopping back down on the couch.

"Oh my gosh, it's our yearbook from middle school," I said.

I opened it up and felt a wave of nostalgia as I thumbed through its pages.

"From eighth grade."

"I remember," I replied looking at all the faces, some I had forgotten all about and others I remembered like it was yesterday.

He smiled, "You remember what I wrote in the back?"

"Of course, I never forgot," I said looking to him.

He took it from my hands and flipped to the very last page. And then he read it to me. To *us*.

Rana,

To a really beautiful mature women that I've known for a long time. We really hit it off this year and you've always been there when I needed "ya". And you still cant tell anybody ~~from~~ about those inside jokes. And dont worry about me leavin, you know I'll drive over to your house. And when I'm in my 20's I'll come back and find you & marry you, like I said I would, Hey. I'm goin to the pro's to. Probably Baseball. But call me sometime

right.

love.

Ryan delivered on every promise he made to me in this letter (including going pro for baseball – he played briefly for the Cincinnati Reds farm system). A true man of his word.

I listened, in awe at Ryan's foresight, even as a fourteen-year-old. Until now, neither of us had ever brought up what he had written to me that day; the promise he made me.

"How did you know we'd end up together?" I asked.

"I'm not sure, I just...did," he smirked.

I smiled back and leaned in for a kiss. His lips gently pressed against mine and I recalled the day he boldly stole my first kiss after school. The same lips that gave me my first kiss would also give me my last, I could hardly believe it.

I know that our love is something that spans beyond the two of us. It was our destiny, and it was written long ago.

A small snippet of our big day (and yes, my BFF made our cake!).

The dress my mom, Nonna Petitti and I designed and made. The bodice is from my other Nonna Mancini's original wedding dress.

FINAL WORDS

Our love has certainly been a fairytale in a lot of ways. And because we live in the real world, we've also had our ups and downs. But at the end of the day, I'm with the most loving man I could possibly imagine for myself. And I'm a better person just by being his partner. My hope is you find the same thing in your love.

What I love most about writing this book is that it prompts others to share their love stories with me. And I adore hearing from my readers! Connect with me on social media @ChicTravelingMama or email me directly Rana@ChicTravelingMama.net.

Lastly, if you've enjoyed this book, please leave an Amazon review, they're important for authors and I read every single one!

Recently on set in Toronto.

Made in the USA
Lexington, KY
19 April 2019